The Ghost of
Thomas Kempe

The Ghost of Thomas Kempe

Illustrated by
Antony Maitland

mammoth

First published in Great Britain 1973
by Heinemann Young Books
Published 1992 by Mammoth
Reissued 2000 by Mammoth
an imprint of Egmont Children's Books Limited,
a division of Egmont Holding Limited,
239 Kensington High Street, London W8 6SA

Text copyright © Penelope Lively 1973
Illustrations copyright © Heinemann Young Books 1973
Cover illustration copyright © Sarah Perkins 2000

ISBN 0 7497 0791 7

10 9 8 7 6 5 4 3

A CIP catalogue record for this title
is available from the British Library

Printed and bound in Great Britain
by Cox & Wyman Ltd, Reading, Berkshire

'What's this, then?'

The two men were in the roof of the cottage, working on the attic that was to be made into a bedroom. The floor was white with the plaster they had chipped away from the walls. Cobwebs trickled from the rafters. One of the men, prising a chunk of rotten wood from the window frame, had let fall a small bottle wedged behind. It broke as it touched the floor: greenish glass, with a sediment clinging to it.

The other man touched it with his foot. 'That's old glass, that is.'

'This is an old place. Look at the thickness of that wall. And the chimney goes right up through.'

The man who had dropped the bottle pushed the fragments of glass to one side, among plaster chunks, and curls of old wallpaper patterned with green leaves. Whistling, he began to cut new wood for the window frame.

'There's a gap under that frame. Where the old wood come out.'

'I'll plaster it over.'

'Nice view out of there. Straight over to the church.'

'And the lock-up. Remind you to keep your nose clean, eh?' The men laughed.

'This room's not been used in years, I'd say.'

'No. There was an old couple lived here before. Didn't need the space. We had to break the door down, first time I come up here with Mrs Harrison, to see what work had to be done on it. Nailed up, it was. The dust was that thick it was like no one had been up here in a hundred years.'

'Make a nice room when we've done.'

'For the boy, she said. Room of his own, like.'

'We'll get cleared up. I want to get down to the allotment to-night.'

They began to stack tools, sweep the rubbish into a corner. Dust swirled like smoke in the shaft of evening sunlight from the small window: rolls of it drifted over the floor, clinging to the men's feet and overalls.

'Draughty in here.'

'We'll have to see to that window. It wants refitting.'

The men picked up their tools and clattered down the wooden stairs. The door banged behind them, shaking more plaster from the walls, and their footsteps went away down the street. In the room, there was a gathering of air: it bunched and compressed into little winds that nosed the mounds of wallpaper, rustled them, and set the windows faintly rattling. Then it subsided, and the room was quiet: empty.

I

James Harrison and his mother turned out of Ledsham's main street into a lane that ran between terraced cottages. The lane ended abruptly at a gate and became a footpath which disappeared in a landscape of fields and trees, ridged with the dark lines of hedges. Their own cottage stood at the end: the last house in Ledsham. It was called East End Cottage and they had been living there for two weeks.

James walked five paces behind his mother, carrying her shopping basket, which he disliked because it banged against his bare legs and scratched him where the cane was broken. Also it had things like ladies' tights and cabbages sticking out of it, which was embarrassing. Tim, the dog, walked ten paces behind James. James looked back at him and tried to imagine him as one of those large, shaggy, responsible-looking dogs that carry folded-up newspapers and shopping baskets. Tim, squat, square and mongrel, grinned back, independent and unobliging.

They passed under low eaves encrusted with swallows' nests, hanging above front doors that opened straight on to the pavement. Behind each small window were huge plants in pots, dimly green behind the glass, as though seen underwater, shielding murky rooms. In one, a ginger cat gloated at Tim, who scrabbled at the wall in a frenzy of frustration and evil language.

'Make him come,' said Mrs Harrison. 'He'll give us a

bad name. Since we seem to have acquired him now, whether we like it or not.'

Tim had arrived at East End Cottage shortly after the Harrisons. He had been found sitting outside the back door, looking pathetic and homeless, had been fed, and within days had installed himself firmly within the house, establishing his rights and ingratiating himself with Mrs Harrison who he was quick to identify as the source of food. He was, clearly, a dog with a long, complicated and mysterious past. Sometimes other people in the village glanced at him curiously, as though they could not quite place him. The postman said he could swear he'd lived at the butcher's at one time and Mr Harrison said grimly that didn't surprise him in the least.

James looped the belt of his jeans through Tim's collar and pulled him away. Tim immediately drooped his stumpy tail and assumed his ill-treated dog pose, for the benefit of an old lady watching from over the street.

'Huh,' said James. 'You don't fool me, you know.' He caught up with his mother.

'Anything for tea?'

'Food,' said Mrs Harrison. 'As usual. I'll have the basket now. Thank you for carrying it.'

'Not at all,' said James politely. He had just embarked on a policy of insurance against various crimes he was certain to commit before long, either with or without intending to. His mother gave him a startled look.

They were almost home now. James could see the window of his attic room, staring over towards the church. The cottage was small, square and comfortable: coming to live in it had been like putting on an old coat. It had a sagging slate roof, a bulge at one end where once there had been a bread-oven, huge beams, creaking stairs, and stone floors with interesting cracks from which emerged, at night, large and stately black beetles. James was making a study of the black beetles: it was

4

going to be called *The life Cycle of a British Beetle* by Dr James Harrison, F.R.S., M.P., D.Phil., O.B.E. Helen preferred the new houses in the estate the other side of Ledsham, where she already had a network of friends.

'They've got tiled bathrooms, and fitted kitchens. And carpet all the way up the stairs. You ought to see, Mum.'

'I'm sure they're very enviable, dear. But your father and I rather fancied the cottage.'

Mum could be quite sensible about some things, you had to admit that. It makes you wonder, James thought bitterly, what she had to have Helen for. I mean, when you think of all the people she might have had, and she had to have Helen. Other people's sisters were pretty fearful too, but Helen beat the lot. Tiled bathrooms ... Ugh!

Helen, of course, had never discovered that you could climb the apple tree that overhung the back of the house and get from thence on to the ledge of the chimney stack. And she'd not noticed the possibilities of the rubbish heap at the far end of the orchard, full of stuff chucked out by the workmen, which he had yet to examine properly. And only he and Tim knew about the nettle-covered well by the fence, where, they strongly suspected, there were rats.

They had seventeen apple trees, instead of the lawn and flower-beds favoured by Helen. Splendid apple trees, with writhing twisted branches like a troupe of weird dancers frozen amid the long grass. The trees were sagging now, in autumn, with ripe fruit. Mrs Harrison, who was a practical person, had stuck a blackboard up outside the cottage. They could see it now, as they came towards the gate, propped up against the hedge. It said, in white chalk:

> Bramleys—5p. per pound
> Worcesters 6p. ” ”
> Windfalls 3p. ” ”

BRAMLEYS
WORCCS
5p. PORD
CERS
5p. each
WINDFALS
3p. each
Sorcerie
Astrologie
Geomoncie
Alchemie
Recoverie of
Goodes loste
Physicke

And underneath that it said:

Sorcerie
Astrologie
Geomancie
Alchemie
Recoverie of Goodes Loste
Physicke

Mrs Harrison put down the basket and read it through carefully. 'Very funny,' she said. 'Very witty. Though the spelling is a little archaic, if I may say so. I suppose I was asking for something like that, putting that board up. And now would you mind wiping it off before tea.' She went up the path and into the cottage. From within came the monotonous sound of Helen playing with a friend.

James studied the blackboard. Not Helen, certainly not Helen. Dad? But the blackboard had not been tampered with when Mr Harrison left in the morning, and he would not be back till later. So who, then? Somebody, thought James, bristling, having a go at me. There's that boy down the road. Simon something. Or one of the other boys at school. How did they know all those words, though? You'd have needed a dictionary for that lot. I'm going to have to sort this out, he thought. Later.

He followed Tim round the back of the cottage, remembering some unfinished business they had with a hole between the roots of one of the apple trees. They were trying to see if it was possible to mine one's way right under one of the trees and come up the other side. Tim, whatever his other shortcomings, was always game for that kind of thing: indeed, insofar as it is possible for a dog to do so, he even made suggestions himself.

They did some more work on their hole and then, finding

themselves thwarted by a large root, decided to come in for tea. Helen and her friend, a pale girl with plaits, no doubt from the world of fitted kitchens and carpeted stairs, were already seated at the table. They watched him come in with a disapproving stare.

'That's my brother,' said Helen. The friend nodded sympathetically.

There were scones and swiss roll. James sat down, feeling cheerful and hungry.

'Mother,' said Helen loudly, 'I do think James might wash his hands before he comes in to tea. Specially when I've got a visitor.' Calling Mum 'mother' was a new idea of hers: she thought it elegant. James glared at her.

'Point taken,' said Mrs Harrison. 'Go and wash them, James.'

He stamped up to the bathroom, and washed the backs of his hands, leaving the palms untouched. Helen needn't think she could win a total victory. His face, freckled, thatched with thick, butter-coloured hair, grinned at him from the mirror: he tried out some of his expressions, the bad-man-in-Western sneer, the Cup-Final captain's grin (holding Cup, or rather, tooth-mug, in upstretched arms), the boxing-champion's snarl (quite good, that one, with towel round neck and hair damped back). Overhead, in his bedroom, he heard a thump. That would be Tim, no doubt. He wasn't supposed to go into the bedrooms, since he made untidy nests on the beds, but there was no known way of stopping him. He was believed to have discovered how to open doors.

His mother's voice came up the stairs. 'James! I said "wash", not have a bath. We're waiting.'

He took the towel off hastily, arranged it on top of the half-open door as a Helen-trap, and hurried downstairs, saying 'Coming, mother. Sorry, mother.'

'That'll do,' said Mrs Harrison. 'I'm beginning to feel like

8

a lady in a Victorian novel. Any more of that and I'll get you a frilly shirt and satin knickerbockers.'

Helen and the friend tittered. Something with the bristly texture of a pan-cleaner rubbed against James' leg: it was Tim, dropping hints about the swiss roll. James gave him a puzzled glance. Had he learned to fly, too?

'More cake?' said Mrs Harrison. 'Julia? Helen? No, James, that is the cake, not the slice, if you don't mind. What are you girls planning to do after tea?'

They exchanged looks and began to giggle. 'We'll tell you later,' said Helen, in a heavy whisper. James arranged his face into what he hoped was an expression of deep, seering contempt. That was one of the things about girls—one of the many, many things—this business of going all secret and ridiculous and pretending they were up to something when you knew perfectly well they were too dim to get up to anything at all except some daft business messing about in the kitchen. He sighed deeply, and stared out of the window, with the preoccupied look of someone who has real concerns.

'And you, James? Oh, but you have a job to do, haven't you? That board.'

'We knew it was you,' said Helen. 'We thought it was silly.'

James closed his eyes and assumed an expression of tired resignation.

'Pointless. I s'pose that's why you were late for school.'

James opened one eye and looked balefully at her.

'Not again, James,' said Mrs Harrison.

'And it was all spelt wrong, anyway,' Helen went on.

'All right, then,' said James, goaded beyond endurance. 'Bet *you* don't know what astrology means.'

'I do.'

'What, then?'

'Not telling you,' said Helen.

James said 'Huh'. He fetched the dishcloth from the sink,

9

damped it under the tap, and went out to the gate. Scrubbing the unwanted writing from the board, he thought that whoever had done it had really made rather a good job of it with those curly s's and funny e's. It looked a bit like the writing on old stones, or memorials in churches. All the same, he'd have to find out who it was. You couldn't have people coming along and doing that kind of thing without asking: that was cheek. I'll start with that Simon person, he thought, I bet it was him. He'd noticed him vaguely at school, a short, stumpy boy with immensely thick, round glasses.

He damped the dishcloth a bit more in a puddle and arranged it on the saddle of Helen's bike. Then he set off for Simon's house, which was at the other end of the lane, towards the High Street.

Simon was conveniently available outside his house, lying along the top of a stone wall. His bespectacled face stared down at James like an amiable gargoyle. 'Hello,' he said, in a friendly, unconcealing voice, not at all like someone who has just been responsible for some kind of trick. Unless, of course, he was a skilled actor.

James found himself at a loss. He stared at Simon for a minute, doubtfully, and then said, with less conviction than he had intended, 'Very funny joke. Ha ha.'

'What?' said Simon.

'Very funny. What you wrote on my mum's blackboard. Very humorous.'

'Hang on,' said Simon. He took off his glasses, which were deeply encrusted with dirt, and rubbed them on his shirt-sleeve, as though a clearer view of the world might help him to understand better. He put them on again and said, 'What blackboard?'

'*You* know.'

'No, I don't.'

'The one outside our house.'

'Let's see,' said Simon, sliding down from the wall.

'I've rubbed it off now. Have you got a pencil?'

Simon felt in his pocket and fished out a chocolate label and a slightly chewed biro. James leaned the paper on a brick and wrote, as nearly as he could remember, the words. 'There!'

Simon peered at them thoughtfully, 'It wasn't me,' he said. 'I promise. For a start I don't know what they mean. Except Sorcerie—that's obvious. And Physicke—that's old-fashioned language for medicine. And Recoverie of Goodes loste just means finding things, I suppose. Anyway,' he went on with disarming honesty, 'I couldn't have spelt them.'

'They're spelt wrong, actually,' said James.

'Oh, are they?'

James studied Simon. There are some people you feel inclined to believe, whatever they say, and others you don't: Simon, he felt, belonged to the first lot.

'Honestly?' he said. 'Swear?'

'Swear.'

'Who do you think it was then? Someone from school?'

'I dunno,' said Simon vaguely. 'Might have been.' He seemed to be losing interest in the problem. 'I've climbed your apple trees,' he said. 'Before you came. The people didn't notice. I accidentally ate an apple, too. The best ones are on the tree right at the end.'

'I know,' said James. 'Come on. I'll show you my hole, if you like.'

They walked down the lane together. At the gate James paused and looked suspiciously at the apple-board, but all was as it should be. Tim was sitting outside the gate, staring up at James' bedroom window, making unpleasant growling noises in the back of his throat.

'What's up, Tim?' said James.

'He's saying there's someone he doesn't like in that room,' said Simon.

'It's my room. I bet those stupid girls are in there. Helen's always nosing about. I'll just ... No, not now, or we won't have time for the hole. I'll see about her later.'

They spent a happy hour or so on the hole, and discovered a way round the root. Then they did some climbing and worked out a new route up the north face of the largest apple tree. Finally they lay down in the long grass and ate as many apples as they could comfortably manage, throwing the cores to Tim who ate them all, not because he liked them but because he was a dog who had learned never to let an opportunity pass, lest one regret it later.

'I'll have to go,' said Simon finally.

' 'Bye then. See you.'

'See you.'

There was cauliflower cheese for supper: not one of James' favourites. He tried unsuccessfully to share it with Tim under the table, but Tim, perhaps, had overdone it with the apple cores because he rejected the offerings and circled the kitchen restlessly, as though he had something on his mind. Eventually he went out into the garden, growling.

'Shut the back door, James,' said Mrs Harrison. 'This house is draughty, there's no getting away from it. There's been a cold wind round my feet for the last half-hour.'

'Julia's house is ever so warm,' said Helen. 'It's got central heating.'

'I'd sooner have beetles than central heating,' said James. And mice, he added, but under his breath because that was something he was keeping to himself in case it occurred to anyone that they ought to be trapped.

'Typical,' said Helen. 'Do you know, Mum, he's found some-one else just like him. Even grubbier, if possible. They were up the apple tree together.'

'How nice,' said Mrs Harrison. 'Now you've both got a friend.'

12

James remembered that he still had a score to settle with Helen. He accused her of invading his room. Helen, in exaggerated tones of outrage, said she wouldn't be seen dead in his room. James said he *knew* she'd been there, and it wasn't fair. Both appealed to their mother.

'Stop it, both of you,' said Mrs Harrison. 'I'm a mother, not a referee.'

James, struck with the happy thought of his mother in shorts with a whistle round her neck, began to howl with laughter. Helen glowered at him: she took arguments seriously and liked to pursue them to the bitter end.

'And another thing, Mum, he put a filthy dishcloth on my bike saddle and I sat on it and Julia saw. I mean, it's awfully *embarrassing* in front of my friends.'

'I daresay they've got brothers too,' said Mrs Harrison. 'James, you're to leave your sister alone, do you hear?'

But James had already retreated upstairs.

Sitting on the edge of his bed, undressing, he contemplated his room with satisfaction. It was a jolly good room. The walls and ceilings all sloped wildly in different directions, so that it seemed geometrically impossible that they should all come together in the right way to make up a room at all. The floor was crooked: if you put a marble down it would roll very slowly from one end to the other. You had to stoop a little to see out of the window, but there was a good view, over the rooftops of Ledsham, a clutter of slate and thatch, to the square tower of the church, with swallows dipping round it and the odd little building in the old market place that had once been the village jail and was now the Public Library. There was a table, a chest, and a couple of shelves where James kept his books, his fossil collection, his shells, and various other things, including the clay models he'd made at school last week, two of which, he saw with irritation, had been knocked on to the floor. So she had been up here. Liar.

He rearranged the models and got into bed. He reached under the pillow for his Personal Notebook and began to fill in various details for the day. Under the heading 'Financial Situation', he wrote 'Same as yesterday. I owe Simon 1p. now for winning bet about spitting apple pips farthest. He owes me two sherbet sticks. No pocket money till larder window is paid for.' He turned over the page and put 'Weather good. Wind moderate and coming from west (I think. Unless weathercock on church tower is stuck).' The next page was headed 'Food', and he wrote 'Cottage pie for lunch. Smashing. Three helpings. Cauliflower cheese for dinner. It is the only thing Tim will not eat.' He turned over again, to the page headed 'Future plans'. This was always very full. Now he wrote 'Make complete tunnel from one end of orchard to the other. If successful, send plans to people who are going to build Channel Tunnel. Rig up trap to stop Helen getting into my room. Get hold of a dictionary, and look up "alchemy". Train Tim to carry shopping-baskets.'

Then he put the notebook under the pillow once more, turned the light out, and went immediately to sleep.

During the night he woke feeling cold, and found the eiderdown had been twitched off on to the floor. There was a draught, too, from under the door or somewhere. Crossly, he rearranged the bed, and went to sleep again.

'Has anyone seen my pipe?' said Mr Harrison.

'On the dresser,' said Mrs Harrison, without looking up from the sink.

'Under the cornflake packet,' said Helen, through a mouthful of toast.

Mr Harrison walked over to the dresser, stood there, returned to the table, lifted the cornflake packet and put it down again, and then said, 'Don't let me make a nuisance of myself. Distract people, or anything like that. What's your suggestion, James?'

'Hall table,' said James. 'Is there any more bacon, Mum?'

'Thank you,' said his father. 'Is that a hard fact, or merely an informed guess? Don't bother to answer.' He went out of the room and could be heard creaking across the hall.

'Before you disappear altogether I want you to do an errand for me this morning, James,' said Mrs Harrison.

'Yes, Mum. Certainly, Mum.' It was just possible, he'd decided, that a sustained policy of helpfulness might do something to cancel out the larder window.

'I want you to take Helen's prescription along to the chemist for me. I forgot it yesterday.'

Indignation overcame diplomacy. 'Gosh, Mum, why can't she do it? It's not fair. After all, it's her cough, isn't it?'

'She's been invited to the Robinsons' for the day. She won't have time. Did you find it?' Mr Harrison had returned.

'I did not.'

'Oh dear, James and I will have a hunt for it while you're out.'

'Slavery,' said James under his breath. Helen was smirking at him across the table.

'What's that, James?' said Mr Harrison.

'Nothing, Dad. I was just saying to Helen I hoped she'd have a lovely day.'

'Ooh ...' began Helen.

'Well, I'm off now,' said Mr Harrison. 'Goodbye.'

' 'Bye, Dad. Well, I s'pose I might as well go and get this weedkiller for Helen. I mean cough mixture.'

'Here's the prescription. Be careful of it.' Mrs Harrison fished the piece of paper out of the teapot where spare buttons, loose change and vital documents were kept. James stuffed it into his pocket, and went out into the early-morning bustle of Ledsham. It was a very old place, half way between a village and a small town, and had, somehow, the air of being dwarfed by the present. New housing estates were mushrooming now on two sides of it, but the centre remained as it must always have been with the houses and streets a size smaller than the houses and streets of a modern town. Lorries, and even the tops of cars, rode parallel with the upstairs windows of the terraced cottages: the streets were too narrow, and the corners too abrupt, for modern traffic, creating the most enthralling traffic-jams. James watched one now, with interest, as the Huntley and Palmer lorry became inextricably tangled up with a tractor and trailer at the main crossroads. There were six pubs, most of them called The Swan, two butchers, no supermarkets, a hairdresser's called Style and Elegance, and a huge, brand-new, plate-glass and concrete comprehensive school, where, nonetheless, most of the names on the register were the same as those in the records of Births, Deaths and Marriages in the church which went back nearly five hundred years.

The streets had brief, sensible names that talked about the town's past: Acre End Street, Abbey Way, Pound Lane. Lined with small, honey-coloured houses, they pointed away into the countryside, into green, rivery, elm-scattered Oxfordshire.

The tractor and the Huntley and Palmer lorry sorted themselves out and James moved on, regretfully. It was Saturday: the day stretched ahead, not set aside for anything in particular, full of possibilities. I might get on with the hole, James thought, or I might see if Simon's got any better ideas, or I might go and see those archaeologist people who're digging up something at that farm, or I might . . . He caught sight of his own face in a cottage window, and paused to make his chattering-ape grimace at it. Music, floating down from a radio in a room above, reminded him of his Famous Conductor act. He stood on a brick to get a better view of himself, raised his baton (or rather, bent straw from gutter) nodded curtly to the orchestra, and flung out his arms to bring in the three thousand massed violins. He was just pushing the hair out of his eyes after a particularly frenzied bit when the astonished face of an elderly man behind the glass reminded him that he was not alone. He got down off the brick hastily.

The chemist's was full of people. He had to wait his turn. Once, he spotted Simon passing the window, sandwiched between his parents, wearing clean, going-to-visit-relations clothes. Poor old Simon. He waved wildly to attract his attention, and then tried to mime a message of sympathy and see-you-tomorrow-when-it's-all-over. Simon was swept past before he could respond.

'When you've quite finished,' said the lady behind the counter heavily. 'I'm waiting.'

'Oh, sorry,' said James. 'My Mum says can she have this please.' He felt in his pocket for the prescription and handed it over.

The assistant turned away, glancing at it. Then she stopped, frowned, and looked more closely.

'Here,' she said. 'Someone's been fooling about with this. I can't take it like this.'

'Let's have a look,' said James.

She handed the prescription back to him. Sure enough, at the top it said, in Doctor Larkins' neat handwriting, 'Mist. Pect. Inf., Tinct. lpecac. m II, Syrup Squill m V, Syrup Tolu. m V, 1 teaspoonful t.d.s. to be taken twice daily,' which presumably meant cough mixture. But somebody had drawn a bold blue line through that, in biro, and written underneath, in the same crabbed, old-fashioned looking writing as the words on the apple blackboard, 'Take the leaves of Lungwort, which is a herb of Jupiter, boile them and make of them a syrupe which will much ease a coughe. I counsell thee also to saye certeine charmes over the sicke childe.'

James gaped at it.

'You've got a joker in your house,' said the assistant, looking hard at him. 'Next, please.'

James went out on to the pavement, still staring at the prescription. The matter of the blackboard had been one thing —there were various explanations for that which were quite possible— but this was something else altogether. There were only four people who knew that prescriptions were kept in the old black teapot: his father, his mother, Helen and himself. It was unthinkable that either of his parents would tamper with something as important as a prescription, even for an elaborate joke. And the same went for Helen, who took her health with deadly seriousness. That left . . .

Me, thought James. And I didn't do it. He began to walk home, very slowly.

At the corner of the lane he stopped. He was in a very awkward situation: there was just no getting away from the fact. If he showed the prescription to his mother she would undoubtedly reach the same conclusion as he had just done. But she didn't know that he hadn't done it.

And the trouble is, he thought, that I'm the sort of boy who might do that sort of thing. And she knows that. Because it's the sort of thing I do sometimes.

Bother.

He worried about what to do all the way back to the cottage. And underneath that worry there was the other matter of who *had* done it. Because he was going to have to get to the bottom of it. It looked suspiciously as though someone was getting at him, and he wasn't going to be got at, not without doing something about it.

He took a deep breath and marched into the kitchen, where he could hear his mother slapping a wooden spoon around in

19

a bowl, and humming. At least Helen wouldn't be about—there was that to be thankful for.

Fifteen minutes later he was sitting on the end of his bed, feeling injured and resentful. She hadn't believed him. As she'd pointed out, with some justification, he had to admit, who else could it have been? And the more vehement and truthful he'd tried to be, the more red-faced and untruthful-sounding he'd become, which was most unfair. In fact the whole thing was bitterly unfair: one didn't mind being told off and punished for things one had done—at least not much —but when it came to something that one hadn't even done ... Glowering, he determined to find out who this rotten person was if it was the last thing he did. He ground the toe of his plimsoll into the rug by his bed: the whole promising day had collapsed in ruins around him. He was to spend it helping her clear out the old shed at the back of the cottage, as a penance. When he'd tidied his room.

Tim was pacing round and round the floor with the hairs along his spine lifted in a dark ridge, exactly as he behaved when in the neighbourhood of the well in the orchard. All of a sudden he sat down on his haunches, facing the table where James did his homework, and barked.

'Shut up,' said James. 'There aren't any rats up here.'

Tim batted his short tail to and fro and barked again. Then he bared his teeth and growled.

'Oh, cut it out,' said James irritably. He began to make the bed, rolling his pyjamas into a ball and stuffing them under the pillow, and smoothing the counterpane over the disaster area underneath. Only an experienced eye would spot the deception, and with any luck his mother wouldn't come up before tonight. He went round the room picking up things that were on the floor and arranging them in piles elsewhere, which is always the most effective way of making a room appear tidy. Even as he did so a pen rolled off the table behind him, and some papers fluttered in the breeze from the open window. How could he be expected to keep his room tidy when things moved about by themselves, huh?

He picked the pen up—his good red biro it was, and it looked as if someone had been mucking about with it—and put it back on the table. All of a sudden something caught his eye. Some red writing on a sheet of paper laid on top of his project book. Not his writing. He picked it up: it looked horribly familiar. Not *again* ...

It said:

> Tell thy father that if he would knowe who hath stollen his pipe he should take a sieve & hange itt from a payre of sheeres & when he name the person he suspecteth the sheeres will turne. Or if he preferre he may use the crystalle. I have been about the towne & I am muche displeased for there are manie who do usurpe my worke & professe to find thieves & give physicke & thou hast in this verie dwellynge a machine which tells if there will be muche sunshine or no. We will be verie busie, thou & I.

The writing was spidery, as though the pen had slid about. At the bottom of the page there was a further line, which said petulantly 'I lyke not this quill'.

James sat down on the bed, because his legs suddenly felt a bit odd. He read it through three times, while Tim went to sleep in the patch of yellow sunlight from the window. Then he did some hard thinking, and came up with some conclusions. Namely, that the writing had not been there when he got up that morning, that therefore it had been done since then, and it could not have been done by either his father or by Helen, since both had come downstairs before he had and had left the house without going up again.

So either his mother was playing an elaborate joke on him —so elaborate, indeed, that one would have to think she had gone absolutely barmy—or someone else had been in the house. Which was rather a creepy idea.

And there were other things, too. Tim, barking at the empty air. Thumps, from a room with nobody in it.

He folded the paper up carefully and put it in the wallet where he kept various important things, like old programmes and entrance tickets and his swimming certificates. Then he went downstairs, feeling thoughtful.

Mrs Harrison and James spent the rest of the morning dragging junk out of the shed. It was to be made into a workshop and storeroom. It was not so much a shed, really, as a part of the house, since it was built of the same stone and adjoined it, though the old slate roof had fallen in and been replaced with corrugated iron. Mrs Harrison said she supposed it must once have been a cowshed. The job was less tedious than James had expected, since there were all kinds of interesting things in the shed, like immensely old and complex mousetraps, ancient agricultural implements of tortuous design whose purpose could not even be guessed at, a calendar dating from the first World War, and (joy of joys!) a tin helmet and a gas-mask. James cheered up considerably as the morning progressed. He also probed his mother, cautiously, talking loudly about sieves, shears, and crystals, and asking her how you spelt 'physicke'. To none of this did she respond in any way, except to say would he kindly stop chuntering on about nothing and get on with what he was supposed to be doing.

Finally he said, as casually as he could manage, 'By the way, Mum, did anyone come in while I was at the chemist? Just kind of blow in and wander up the stairs?'

'No,' she said. 'Nobody blew or wandered. Would you like to put all this stuff in a wheelbarrow and take it down to the rubbish heap? No, on second thoughts, dig a hole and bury it.'

Digging the hole took up most of the afternoon. As a professional hole-digger, James took the matter seriously. He made it good and deep, and as he dug it soon became clear that he was digging up someone else's much more ancient rubbish heap, since he kept uncovering bits of broken china and pottery and innumerable small bones, as well as the stems and bowls of clay pipes. One of the advantages of living in a house which had been lived in for a pretty long time was that other people's very interesting rubbish was never far away. After an hour or so he had unearthed a whole sequence of domestic break-ages, from eighteenth-century wine-bottles through flowery Victorian cups to twentieth-century Woolworth's blue and white china. The bones, too, would need to be classified: most of them were clearly the remains of long-past Sunday dinners, or the buried treasure of Tim's ancestors, but some at least, he thought hopefully, might turn out to be human. At last he decided the hole would do, and dragged the wheelbarrow to the edge in order to tip the contents into it. Just as he was about to do so he caught sight of a curled piece of wire pro-truding from the side of the hole: he stooped down and gave it a tug. It came out with a shower of loose soil and revealed itself to be one arm of a very ancient pair of spectacles. He examined this trophy with much pleasure: the lenses had gone, but the frame was intact—thin, rusty wire with very small eye-pieces, not unlike the National Health ones that Simon wore. He put them in his pocket.

By the evening, after a day of reasonably amicable relations with his mother, James felt that the matter of the prescription had been dropped. At least, it was not mentioned again. But as far as he himself was concerned it was not over at all, he had yet to find out who was responsible. He was not going to go on taking the blame for things he hadn't done. Huh ...

At supper Mr Harrison said, 'Oh, by the way, I hope you didn't waste a lot of time looking for my pipe. It was in my jacket pocket after all.'

James and his mother looked at each other. 'I must confess

we forgot all about it,' said Mrs Harrison.

'Nobody stole it?' said James.

'I never suggested anybody had.'

'What's *he* been doing all day?' said Helen, eyeing James with distaste.

'Oh, nothing much,' said James airily. 'Mum took me to a circus this afternoon, and we had home-made ice-cream for lunch. Three helpings each. And this morning we went swimming. It was rather a dull day really. You didn't miss much.'

Helen's eyes grew large and shiny, the signal of approaching tears. She put down her knife and fork and began, furiously, 'Oh, it's not fair ... Just when I wasn't here ...'

'Helen,' said Mr Harrison, with a sigh, 'we all know that living with James can be very trying. But it does help to develop a resistance to some of his more flagrant lines of deception.'

Helen picked up her knife and fork again, with a baleful look at James, who grinned back.

'He's been here all day,' said Mrs Harrison. 'As a matter of fact he was being punished ...'

'Crumbs!' said James, leaping to his feet and rushing to the window. 'What's that!'

It worked. Tim flew from under the table and rushed at the door, barking wildly and pulling the cloth half off the table. A glass of water fell over, everybody tried to mop it up and in the general commotion the rest of Mrs Harrison's remark was lost.

'Sorry,' said James, 'thought I saw someone in the garden. Mistake.'

His father gave him the hard stare of a man who had not been taken in, and went through to the sitting-room. James followed, hurriedly turning on the television to forestall any further remarks.

Television has many virtues, not the least of them being,

James thought, that it provides a continuous noise to paper over a potentially unreliable situation. The Harrisons settled down for the evening: once, Helen said, 'Where's my new cough mixture?' but her mother's reply was drowned in a burst of gunfire from the Mexican border.

'Ssh,' said James. 'This is good.'

He and Helen lay on their stomachs, side by side, with Tim between them. Tim sat with his head between his paws, facing the television set, eyes half-closed, occasionally twitching. He clearly thought the television screen to be a window beyond which there was a real and thrilling world from which he was excluded, peopled with fleeing horses, other dogs, and a host of wild animals. Occasionally, when things got too much for him, he would hurl himself against the glass in an abortive attempt to chase these elusive creatures. He was believed by James and Mr Harrison to appreciate a good Western.

'Bed,' said Mrs Harrison, at last.

'In a minute,' said James and Helen in unison.

'As soon as the news is over, then.'

The news ended. The weather forecast began. 'Tomorrow will be cloudy and dull in most parts, with light to moderate winds. Temperatures will be around ...'

There was a loud crash from the sideboard. Everybody looked round. The blue vase was lying on the floor in pieces.

'I didn't touch it,' James said quickly. 'I was over here.'

'Nor me,' said Helen. Both children looked at their mother with expressions of deep virtue.

'How very peculiar,' said Mrs Harrison, picking up the pieces. 'Luckily it's one I've never cared for. A wedding present.'

'How on earth did it fall off by itself?' said Helen.

'Small local earthquake,' said their father with a yawn. 'Very frequent in this part of Oxfordshire. Up, both of you.' He picked up the newspaper.

James and Helen climbed the stairs slowly, pausing on every step to argue about who was to use the bathroom first. At the top, Helen gave in unexpectedly.

'You have it. Anyway, you need it most,' she added as an after-thought. Then, 'I say, it was funny about that vase, wasn't it?'

'Mmm,' said James, abstractedly.

'Didn't you honestly do it? Not with a string or something?'

'I jolly well did not.'

'All right, all right. I just wondered.'

James, feeling in his pocket for the various objects he had brought in from his hole, felt the rustle of a piece of paper and remembered. For a moment there flitted around in his head the notion of telling Helen about it, even showing her, telling her about the prescription ... There were times when she could be almost human, and he needed help. Then common-sense prevailed: this wasn't the kind of thing you let a mere girl in on, least of all Helen. He creaked up the stairs to his room.

He was a long time getting to bed. First of all he had to clear a shelf for his new treasures: the spectacle frame, the best of the clay pipes (one, indeed, intact except for an inch or so of stem), the pottery sequence, and various buttons and pieces of bone. He was planning a small exhibition, to be called 'Three Hundred Years of Domestic Life in an Oxford-shire Cottage'. Then, when he'd done that there was the note-book to be filled in (under 'Future Plans' he wrote in block capitals FIND OUT WHO IS PLAYING TRICKS ON ME AND JOLLY WELL SORT HIM OUT), and then at last he was able to get into bed.

He was lying there, telling himself a long and elaborate story about a shipwreck in which he was all the characters by turn, when it suddenly appeared to him that all was not right with the mirror above the table. There was writing on it. He shot out of bed and bounced across the room. Oh *no* ...

There was a further message, scrawled greasily on the mirror in (oh, horror!) his mother's lipstick. James read it with a mixture of indignation and mounting amazement.

Wee must take paines to informe thy neighboures that I doe once more practise my arte and cunninge in this howse. There is much businesse for us in the towne: I fancie manie doe practise witcherie. Tell thy familie they shall knowe what the weather will be from me & not from that eville machine or I will breake more pots. I perceive thou hast dygged up my spectacles & my pipe. It was my first apprentice loste them in the yarde: he was a scoundrell & a lazie fellow & I had often cause to beate him. Take care that thou serve me better.

3

Surprisingly, James slept well. When he woke in the morning the church bells were ringing and the streets were Sunday-ish and quiet, with people cleaning cars instead of driving them and old ladies walking past in gloves and hats. For a moment he couldn't think what it was that nagged somewhere in his head, like a forgotten message or an undiscovered crime, and then he caught sight of the writing on the mirror, and everything came back with a rush. The writing had lost its initial impact now and merely looked scruffy. He rubbed it off with a handkerchief and got back into bed again to think about things.

Sorcerie, astrologie, physicke ...

Thou hast dygged up my spectacles ...

He's got a very weird way of saying things, this person. Old-fashioned. Unless it's somebody putting it on, but it doesn't sound like that.

Nobody but me knows about the spectacles, because as it happens I didn't show them to anyone. Therefore they must have been his spectacles, or he couldn't have known about them.

If someone has spectacles, they are a real person. But those are very old specs.

It was my first apprentice lost them in the yard ...

The person who's writing these messages, thought James carefully, is someone who once lived in this house. He's getting

28

in, somehow, without anyone noticing, and doing it. To have a go at me. For some reason. Because he's barmy or something.

He's getting in, and wandering around, and doing all this, and there are four of us living here and none of us have noticed him.

'No,' he said out loud, 'No.' He got out of bed and dressed, slowly.

Tim goes mad every time anyone comes near the house. Postmen, and milkmen. He'd know. But he has been barking. At nothing.

He said firmly, aloud, 'It's impossible. There aren't such things!' and went downstairs.

'Who lived here before us, Mum?'

'Oh, it was an elderly couple. A Mr and Mrs Rivers.'

'Where did they go?'

'To Scotland, I think it was. They were going to live with their daughter. Mr Rivers had bad arthritis. He couldn't get about much.'

James said, 'Had they lived here long?'

'Ages,' said Mrs Harrison. 'Most of their lives, I think.'

'They haven't been back lately, have they? Dropped in?'

'No, of course not. Why are you so interested in them all of a sudden?'

'I'm not,' said James. 'It doesn't matter.'

It was like knowing you'd done something wrong. You skirted round the problem, and pretended it wasn't there in the hope that it would just go away, and then there it was again, sticking out and tripping you up so that you couldn't ignore it any more.

Somebody is doing this. But they can't be.

Therefore ...

'There's something wrong with James,' said Helen. 'He hasn't said anything for ten minutes.'

Mrs Harrison said, 'Are you feeling all right, James?'

'Yes, thanks.'

'Perhaps he's getting something,' said Helen. 'Measles. There's measles at school.'

'He's had them.'

'It would be just like him to be the first person to get them twice. I mean, when you think of some of the things he's done. Falling through the bathroom ceiling and being the only boy on the school outing to get his arm stuck in a grating so they had to call the Fire Brigade ...'

'It wasn't my fault the loft didn't have a proper floor, was it? And how could I help it if I dropped my sherbet stick through the drain and the stupid bars were made too narrow?' said James belligerently.

'Personally,' said Mr Harrison, 'I always think it better to draw a veil over James' past. May I have the marmalade please?'

James got up. 'I'm going to see Simon.'

'Be sensible.'

'Yes.'

Be sensible. Nothing, he thought grimly, walking down East End Lane, was very sensible at the moment. Nothing made any sense unless you explained it in a way that most people would say wasn't even possible.

Simon was in a less amiable frame of mind than on their first meeting. He had spent yesterday visiting an aunt, it seemed. A particularly clean aunt, who also had strong opinions about noise. Simon had spent all day, he said, being quiet and keeping his feet off things. He claimed that he had sat in total silence on a sofa for three hours.

'With a tie on. And new shoes.' He scowled at James through thickly smeared glasses, as though he might be in some way to blame for this ordeal.

'Not three hours,' said James. 'Nobody could do that. It

couldn't be done. They'd die or something.'

'I nearly did,' said Simon gloomily.

'Listen, I want to talk to you.'

'Go on, then.'

James unfolded his story, incident by incident, repeating the text of the messages as best he could. When he had finished he looked at Simon expectantly.

There was a silence. Then Simon said, 'I think someone's having you on.'

'They can't be. I've told you. About the glasses and all that.'

'Your sister?'

'My sister isn't clever enough to think of it. Not that old-fashioned writing and everything.'

'But who could it be?'

'It's someone who lived in the house once.'

'A real person?'

'Real,' said James, 'once.'

There was a pause. Simon said cautiously, 'Once?'

'Once.'

'You mean,' said Simon, 'not real now?'

'That's right.'

Simon hunched his nose. It was a thing he did every few minutes to push his glasses up again. He said, 'If a person was real once but not now, but they're still going on doing things, then they're a ghost.'

'Yes,' said James.

Simon was silent for a moment. He looked away, blinked, looked back at James and said, 'You think it's a ghost that's doing all this?'

'There isn't anything else I can think. Is there?'

'I didn't *think* I believed in ghosts,' said Simon.

'Neither did I. But I haven't got much choice now, have I?'

Simon said, 'Are you *sure* there isn't someone getting in?'

'Quite sure,' said James coldly. 'I've told you.'

'It's a bit weird, isn't it? I mean, you don't often hear about people having trouble with ghosts, do you?'

'Maybe it's not a thing they talk about. I can see why.'

'You don't see headlines in the paper, after all. MAN COMPLAINS OF GHOST NUISANCE.'

James put his hands in his pockets and began to walk away.

'I'm going. You can come if you want but I don't specially care.'

'I'll come,' said Simon cheerfully. He was the sort of person with whom it is difficult to prolong a disagreement, and after a while James' irritation began to ebb away as they wandered around Ledsham together. They did some exploring in the churchyard until chased away by the Vicar, drifted round the cobbled square and speculated about whether or not prisoners in the lock-up might or might not have been able to escape from the small barred windows at the top ('They'd have to be jolly thin,' said James. 'Half starved. I mean, I know about getting stuck between bars. I'll tell you about it sometime. It was quite good fun really.') Finally they ended up at the field just beyond the outskirts of the village where some archaeologists were excavating a Bronze Age settlement. It wasn't very interesting: two or three people in shirt-sleeves were digging small round holes and sorting through enormous piles of stones and earth, but they were getting enviably dirty in the process. The boys thought it must be a pretty nice kind of job, being paid to dig holes all day: they offered to help, with winning smiles, but were rejected.

'Anybody'd think we were likely to break things, or get things muddled up,' said James resentfully. 'We were only being helpful.'

They walked slowly home, past the school, the fire station, the pubs, the butcher's, the chemist's. James introduced Simon to a game he sometimes played. You walked along quite ordinarily except that you pulled your face into the most extravagant expression you could manage—horror, or fear or joy or anything you fancied. The game was to see how many people noticed. Very few did. You could walk the length of the High Street looking like a zombie and the odds were that no one would bat an eyelid. This, James had worked out to himself, was because as far as most grown-ups were concerned, children were invisible, unless the grown-ups happened to be school-teachers or to have a particular reason for being interested in the child concerned, such as being its parent. For most people, children were something they were so used to seeing around, like lamp-posts or pillar-boxes, that they never really looked at them. Just like dogs pay no attention to people, only to other dogs. Simon was impressed with this theory: he put it to the test, and found it to be true.

They went round the corner into Abbey Road, and past the police station. They paused for a moment to read the notice board. It was a dull notice board: no *Wanted* posters, no sinister criminal faces, front and profile, no Rewards Offered. Merely old, mildewed warnings about dog licences and rear lights on bicycles. And, today, something else.

It was tacked to the wooden frame of the notice board with a rusty nail. Almost before James had read it he knew what was coming. The writing was larger this time, and the letters rather more carefully formed. It was obviously intended to be a notice, or, more precisely, an advertisement. It said:

For the discoverie of goodes loste by the crystalle or by booke and key or with the sieve & sheeres seeke me at my dwellynge which lyes at the extremetie of East Ende Lane. I have muche skille also in such artes as alchemie, astronomie etc. & in physicke & in the seekynge out of wytches & other eville persons. My apprentice, who dwells at the same howse, will bring me messages.

It was signed, rather flamboyantly, with much swirl and flourish:

Thos. Kempe Esq. Sorcerer.

'There!' said James, with a mixture of triumph and despair. 'There! Now do you believe me?'

Simon took his glasses off, scrubbed round them with his fingers and read the notice for a second time. 'Well,' he said cautiously.

'Well what?'

'Somebody could have put it there.'

'Such as who?'

'I don't know.'

'Such as me, perhaps?' said James in a freezing voice.

'No. Not you. You've been with me all morning. You know something?'

James didn't answer.

'If anyone sees it,' Simon went on amiably, 'they might sort of connect it with you. Because it mentions your house.'

James' anger gave way to alarm. 'What shall I do?'

Simon glanced up and down the street. There was no one in sight. The police-station windows stared blankly down at them.

'Take it off. Quickly.'

James hesitated. Then he darted forward, tweaked the notice from the nail and began to walk quickly away down the road, stuffing it in his pocket. Simon caught him up.

'Let's have another look.'

Pulling the notice out again, James saw with indignation that his own red biro had been used once more, and a page from his exercise book. He tore it into very small pieces and put it in a litter basket by the bus stop.

'Whoever he is, this person,' said Simon, 'he's got some pretty funny ideas, hasn't he? Jiggery-pokery with sieves and whatnot to find out who stole things. He'd make a pretty rotten policeman. And leaves for medicines and all that. It

34

wouldn't work—not now there's penicillin and things.'

'He just wants things done like they were in his time,' said James. 'With him doing them. And me helping.'

'Oh,' said Simon. 'I see.' He sounded very polite. Too polite.

James said, 'You don't believe he's a ghost, do you?'

'I didn't say I didn't.'

'But you don't.'

'I kind of half do and half don't,' said Simon with great honesty. 'I do when I'm with you but I think if I was by myself I wouldn't.'

They walked on for a few minutes in silence. Then Simon said, 'What are you going to do? I mean, whatever it is or whoever it is he keeps getting you into trouble.'

'I know. And I'm getting fed up with it. What *can* I do?'

'If he is—what you think,' said Simon, 'there's one thing you could try.'

'What?'

'Ask him to stop it.'

James stared. 'Talk back to him?'

'That's it. Worth trying anyway.'

'Yes. I s'pose it might be.' Somehow that had not occurred to him. But, when you stopped and thought about it, there was no reason why this should be a one way conversation. If he was here, this Thos. Kempe, Sorcerer, making a right nuisance of himself, then the best thing might well be to talk straight back at him. Maybe that was all that was needed. Just explain quietly and firmly that this sort of thing really wouldn't do, and he'd see reason and go away. Back where he came from, wherever that might be.

Feeling rather more hopeful about the future James parted from Simon at his gate and went home for lunch.

A feeling of dissatisfaction hovered around the house. Mrs Harrison was suffering one of her attacks of hay-fever, which made her red-eyed and irritable. Mr Harrison had fallen over a bucket of water standing in the porch, and was resignedly mopping up the mess as James arrived. He followed James into the kitchen, carrying bucket and cloth, which he dumped down by the sink.

'I don't want to interfere with the housekeeping arrangements,' he said, 'but I must point out that the best place for a full bucket of water is not the centre of the front porch.'

'Not guilty,' said his wife, sneezing violently. 'Must have been a child. And don't talk to me about water. I think I'm about to melt as it is.' She began peeling potatoes, with vicious stabs.

'I've only just come in, haven't I?' said James.

'Good gracious!' said Mr Harrison. 'You don't imagine I'd ever suspect it might have been you, do you?' James gave him a suspicious look and went out into the garden to make sure Helen hadn't been interfering with his hole. He found that Tim had located a tributary to the original rat-hole in the drain, and had spent a happy morning digging up a clump of irises. James hastily re-planted them: Tim never seemed to understand that he was only living with them on sufferance as it was and might one day go too far. Mr Harrison had several times said darkly, 'That dog will have to go.'

James patted him kindly. 'You didn't know they weren't weeds, did you?' he said. 'Like you couldn't know Dad still wanted that pair of slippers. Lucky thing I found where you'd buried them, eh?' Tim dropped his head slightly, and bared his teeth in a kind of pink grin, which was the nearest he came to a gesture of affection. He wasn't one of those dogs who climb all over you. He had dignity.

'Come here, sir,' said James sternly. He saw himself and Tim, suddenly, as an intrepid team of criminal-trackers: Harrison of the Yard and his famous trained Rumanian Trufflehound, the Burglar's Scourge. He began to slink along the side of the house with a ferocious scowl on his face, towing a reluctant

36

Tim by the collar. On the other side of that drainpipe lurked the notorious Monte Carlo Diamond Gang, armed to the teeth ...

'Lunch!' shouted Mrs Harrison from the scullery window. Tim shook himself free and bolted for the back door.

After lunch the pewter clouds that had been slowly massing above the village all morning opened up into determined, continuous rain. Mrs Harrison said she felt as though she was being drowned from without as well as within, and went to bed with a book. Mr Harrison went to sleep in an armchair. Helen went to see a friend.

James remembered he had some homework to do. He climbed up to his bedroom, closed the door, and sat down at his table. Tim padded round the room once or twice, jumped up on the bed, swirled the covers around several times until he achieved a satisfactory position, and went to sleep. Outside, the rain drummed on the roof and poured in oily rivers down the window.

James opened his project book, looked at his notes, and began to write. It was a project about ancient Greece, and he was enjoying it. He looked things up, and wrote, and stuck some pictures in, and thought about Alexander the Great, and drew a picture of a vase with blokes having a battle on it, and forgot about everything except what he was doing. Around him, the room rustled occasionally: a piece of paper floated to the floor, and a pen rolled across the table. Tim twitched in his sleep

All of a sudden something nudged James' foot. It was a sheet from his exercise book. He picked it up and read:

I am glad to see thee at thy studies, though I lyke not thy bookes. Where is thy Latin? & where are thy volumes of Astrologie? But to our businesse ... I have putt out the water for people to knowe wee are seeking thieves: it will doe for a crystalle. Thy father's baldnesse could be stayed by bathing with an ointment made from the leaves of Yarrow (a herb of Venus) but there is no cure for thy mother's ailmente of the eyes for it is caused by wytcherie. Nothing will suffice save to seeke out the wytch & bring her to justice. This muste wee doe with all haste.

James swung round in his chair. Then he got up and searched the room, even looking under the bed. There was nothing to be seen, and nothing moved.

He read the note again. The reference to his father's baldness he found particularly annoying. That was cheek, that was. In fact, he thought, he's a proper busybody, that's what he is.

And then he remembered Simon's suggestion. All right then, let's have a go. Let's try talking to him.

He cleared his throat, feeling distinctly foolish at addressing the empty room, even though there was no one to hear, and said 'Er—Mr Kempe.'

Silence. Tim uncurled himself and looked up, yawning.

James took a deep breath and said firmly, 'I'm afraid I can't do the things you want me to do because people don't go in much for sorcery nowadays. I don't think they'd really be very interested. You see we don't use those kind of medicines now because we've got penicillin and that and we've got policemen for finding out if anyone's pinched things and catching thieves and my mother gets hay-fever every year and it really isn't anything to do with witchcraft it's because she's allergic to ...'

There was a loud crash behind him. He whirled round. One of his clay pots had fallen on to the floor and smashed. Even as he looked, a second one raised itself from the shelf, flew across the room, narrowly missing his right ear, and dashed itself against the opposite wall. Tim leapt from the bed and rushed about the room, barking furiously.

'Hey! Stop that!' shouted James.

A gust of wind swept wildly round the room, lifting all the papers on the table and whirling them about the floor. The ink-bottle scuttered to the edge of the table and hung there till James grabbed hold of it with one hand while with the other he made ineffectual dabs at the flying pages from his project book.

'Here! Lay off! Cut it out!'

The door opened and banged itself shut again, twice. The windows rattled as though assaulted by a sudden thunderstorm. The calendar above the bed reared up, twitched itself from the hook, and flapped to the floor. A glass of water on the bedside table tipped over and broke making a large puddle on the mat. Downstairs, James could hear the sitting-room door open, and his father's footsteps across the hall.

'Please!' he squeaked breathlessly, using one hand to steady the chair, which was bucking about like a ship in a storm, while with the other he warded off Volume 1 of *A Child's Encyclopaedia* which had risen from the bookshelf and hurled itself at his head.

'Please! Don't! Look, perhaps I could ...'

Mrs Harrison's bedroom door opened and her voice could be heard saying something loud and not very friendly on the landing. Mr Harrison was coming up the stairs.

The bedcover whisked off the bed, whirled round once or twice, and sank to the floor, engulfing a frantic Tim in its folds.

'All right!' shouted James. 'All right! I'll do it. Anything. If you stop.'

The room subsided. Tim struggled out from under the bedcover and dived for the shelter of the bed. The door opened and Mr Harrison came in. James stood amid the wreckage of his room and waited for the storm to break.

———————————————————

4

James sat hunched gloomily in one of his retreats, Camp 4 on the South Col of the second biggest apple tree, and wrote in his notebook. This was something he normally did in his room, and nowhere else, but somehow after the events of yesterday he no longer wanted to. Apart from anything else, it wasn't private any more, was it? He sucked the stub of the pencil and wrote 'Financial Situation. Worst ever. Broken glass will cost 8p. Bill for cleaning bedcover 25p. No more pocket money till I'm about seventeen, I should think.' Under 'Weather' he wrote, 'Haven't noticed outside weather but conditions in house terrible. Atmosphere stormy.' He brushed a woodlouse off his leg irritably, licked the pencil again and put 'Meals. Didn't get any pudding for supper. Guess why. Helen had two helpings.'

Tim, slumped in the long grass at the foot of the tree, sat up and barked half-heartedly, then yawned and went to sleep. Simon had come round the corner of the house. James put the notebook in his pocket and shouted. Simon climbed up and joined him.

'What's up?'

'Everything. He went mad last night. Threw things about and broke things. And they thought it was me, of course.'

'Who went mad?'

'The sorcerer, of course,' said James shortly.

Simon picked an apple and took a bite out of it. Then he

said 'Oh, him', in a bright interested voice. James was beginning to find this lack of conviction annoying, but he did not, at the moment, feel disposed to start an argument. He stared morosely down through the leaves.

'Why did he?' said Simon.

'Because I did what you suggested and talked to him. I said I wasn't jolly well going to be his apprentice and he got in a rage and threw things. Very bright idea of yours, I must say. Got any more suggestions?'

'Not really,' said Simon, dropping the apple core to Tim. 'If he is what you think he is he's a pretty odd one, anyway, isn't he? Ghosts are supposed to drift around in white sheets, aren't they? Not write letters all the time.'

'I wouldn't know,' said James coldly. 'I don't know anything about them.'

'Neither do I. Why don't we find out? Look them up in a book about ghosts.'

James turned this idea over in his mind. He wasn't sure that it was really very useful, but on the other hand he was rather fond of looking things up and in any case he could think of nothing much else to do.

'All right. Where?'

'The library,' said Simon.

Ledsham Public Library, once the village prison, was a dour, solid little building in the centre of the church square. The high, barred windows and sternly functional appearance were a reminder of its original purpose: inside, however, it was brighter and more welcoming, with whitewashed walls and row upon row of shelves stacked with books. A valiant effort had been made to cater for the many and varied tastes of Ledsham readers. Cookery books and books on *How to Grow Better Chrysanthemums* jostled for space with *The Cathedrals of England* and *The Origins of the Second World War*. Love and crime were rampant on the fiction shelves. In the children's section every book had the appearance of having been well and truly read, or even, in the case of the books for very young children, partially eaten. It was a satisfactory place: familiar, yet inexhaustibly surprising, homely but exotic in its offerings. To plunge into its gloomy entrance was like opening a grocery box and finding it full of Christmas presents.

The librarian, Mrs Branscombe, sat, when she had time to sit, behind a small table laden with card-index boxes. She had been knitting the same jersey for five years, Simon claimed, presumably because most of her time was spent jumping up and down to help the short-sighted, the young, and the confused. Yes, she said, she was sure there must be something on ghosts. She began to hunt along the fiction shelves.

'Not fiction,' said James. 'Not this one, anyway.' Simon looked embarrassed, but Mrs Branscombe had not heard. She found two books of Collected Ghost Stories, and offered them hopefully. The boys looked at each other.

'Actually,' said James, 'what we were thinking of really was something kind of scientific. A sort of Guide to Ghosts. Like Guides to Wild Flowers or Musical Instruments or British Birds.'

Mrs Branscombe said she had a feeling there wasn't anything quite like that. However, being a determined lady, she continued to search, while the boys waited and James, looking up at the small semi-circular barred windows near the ceiling, had a short retreat from real life in which he became a prisoner flung into this dungeon and left there for twenty years on a diet of bread and water flung daily through the window, alone except for the rats (which he tamed) and . . .

'What about this?' said Mrs Branscombe.

James returned to the library with a start. 'What?'

It was an old-fashioned book, called, in gold letters on the spine *Some Reflections Upon the Occult and Supernatural*. The author was, simply, 'A Clergyman.'

'It looks rather out-of-date,' said Mrs Branscombe doubtfully. 'But I don't know what else to suggest. Do you want to take it out, or look at it here?'

'We'll look at it here,' said James. 'Thank you very much.'

They sat on the floor in front of one of the book-cases, and began to look through the book. 'A Clergyman' was not the most stimulating of writers: there were innumerable accounts of ghostly happenings told in very ponderous language, and several chapters on the author's experiences with such things as fortune-telling gypsies, tea-cup reading ladies, and communication with the spirit of a rather uninteresting great-aunt. The only thing which aroused James' interest was a section entitled 'Poltergeists.'

A poltergeist, it appeared, was a particularly riotous kind of ghost. It did not display itself in the conventional way but confined itself to making a great deal of noise, and throwing things. James became very excited.

'That's it!' he said. 'He's one of those. Listen to this. "This species of spirit will frequently manifest itself by means of knocking sounds, the opening and closing of doors, as well as by the movement and even the destruction of plates, cups etc. Such manifestations are often mentioned by our forefathers, indicating a long tradition of such creatures: a medieval demon is said to have thrown stones, beaten against the walls of houses with a hammer, and made accusations concerning thefts, bringing the whole community into an uproar".'

'I s'pose so,' said Simon dubiously. 'It might be. I don't think that book's very scientific though. And it doesn't say anything about writing messages all the time, like you say yours does.'

'I don't *say* mine does. It *is* what he does. You've seen, haven't you? And anyway there's all this stuff about how this clergyman used to sit round a table with his friends and spirits wrote things on bits of paper. Maybe he's got muddled up.'

44

'Mmn,' said Simon. 'Maybe.'

James returned the book to Mrs Branscombe and began to hunt for books on local history. This poltergeist or whatever it was had been a person, once, and he felt suddenly that it might help to know what sort of a person he had been. He pulled out book after book from the 'Oxfordshire' section, searching for something that might throw some light on Thomas Kempe's earthly nature, but without much success. There were two or three histories of Ledsham, but none were very helpful, dealing as they did mainly with the decline and fall of the Abbey for which the village had been renowned in the Middle Ages, and the various buildings of historic interest. There was no mention of the Harrisons' cottage. There was a booklet on the church, which James read through hope-fully, but it told him nothing except that the Perpendicular window on the north side was generally held to be a fine example of the style, the tower had a peal of six bells, and the vault beneath the chancel, believed to contain a number of tombs, had been sealed since the early eighteenth century.

'Come on,' said Simon, fidgeting.

'Coming.' James put the books back, thanked Mrs Brans-combe, and they went out into the square again.

'That wasn't such a bad idea of yours,' said James. 'At least I know now what kind of ghost he is. If that's any help.'

Simon said, 'You know something? I'd like to see him. I've got interested in him.'

'You don't see him. You just hear him. And see what he's done in the way of chucking things around.'

'Well, I wouldn't mind just that. Let's go to your room.'

'It's not exactly an exhibition, you know,' said James. 'It's jolly serious as far as I'm concerned.'

Nevertheless, he allowed Simon to come back to the cottage with him, though without a great deal of enthusiasm. It had taken him ages to clear up yesterday's mess and he had no desire to spark off another demonstration. But he need not have worried. They spent half an hour sitting in his room, without the sorcerer making his presence felt in any way. The room remained perfectly normal and quiet: the books stayed on the shelves, the bedcover was inert, the paper and pencils on the table lay quite still.

Simon became restless. 'It's a bit odd it only happens when you're by yourself,' he said.

'If you think I've made it all up,' said James icily, 'you've got another think coming. Who *wants* all their pocket-money stopped and no pudding and everybody getting in a bad temper with you?'

'All right, all right,' said Simon. 'I was only *saying*.'

They went downstairs. As they passed through the kitchen there was a knock at the front door.

'Could you open it for me?' said Mrs Harrison. 'My hands are all wet. It's only Mrs Verity—I saw her coming up the path.'

Mrs Verity was an elderly widow who lived in the thatched cottage just across the road. She had lived in Ledsham for a long time and knew all about everything: she knew what time the Oxford bus stopped at the corner, where the postman's mother lived, which young man fancied the Vicar's daughter, and where the butcher was going for his holiday. She was, to put it plainly, something of a busybody. And her deepest interest was reserved for those who lived closest to her. She devoted much attention to the Harrisons, trotting up the path at least twice a day.

'Now what?' said Helen. 'This morning she'd run out of sugar. Why don't you pretend to be out, Mum?'

'Because that would be a bit heartless. She's lonely, that's all. And she hasn't got anything to do.'

'She can do my homework,' said Helen, retreating to the other room.

Mrs Verity had come to enquire about Mrs Harrison's hay-fever. And to say that there'd been an accident at the crossroads but no one hurt and Mrs Thompson at the corner shop was expecting again and the Barton boy had been in trouble with the police.

'Not disturbing you, am I, dear?' she said, sitting down uninvited.

Mrs Harrison said that she wasn't and went on beating cake-mix. The boys lurked: there would be a bowl to lick out, they could see.

'And there's been vandalism at the doctor's surgery, I've heard. Shocking, isn't it, all these vandals? His files and papers were all over the place, they say, and things broken.'

'How disgraceful,' said Mrs Harrison.

'That's what I say. And who'd want to do a thing like that, I'd like to know. As nice a man as you could want, that doctor. Ever such a mess it was, they say, but nothing taken. And the police can't find out where they got in. There's no windows broken, and the door was locked.'

James stopped eyeing the cake bowl, and began to listen more carefully. Things broken? Papers all over the place?

Mrs Verity talked on: a flow of statements and observations as unremarkable but demanding as the noise of a dripping tap. James saw his mother glance anxiously at the clock. It had been known to take an hour or more to dislodge Mrs Verity once she was comfortably established. But all of a sudden she stopped talking and shivered.

'I don't know—I feel proper chilly all of a sudden. Isn't there a bit of a draught in here, my dear?'

The curtains whisked. A door banged. Something fell off the table.

'It's this house,' said Mrs Harrison. 'It leaks air, I sometimes think.'

'Ah. These old houses. You can't seem to stop up the cracks

47

properly. What's wrong with your dog, carrying on like that?'

'He thinks there's a mouse,' said James.

Mrs Verity's attention shifted. She had hardly noticed the boys up to this moment. Now she began to hunt in her pockets for a bag of sweets, as though they were some not entirely trustworthy kind of animal, whose confidence must be bought.

'Toffee, dear?'

'Yes, please.'

'It wouldn't have been you two the Vicar was getting so angry with in the churchyard the other day, would it? Walking along the top of the wall?'

The boys tried to look both politely interested but quite uninvolved. Mrs Harrison stopped beating cake-mix and looked hard at them. James stowed the toffee for a moment in the roof of his mouth and said thickly, 'That very high wall?'

'Yes. You could have a nasty accident, falling off that.'

'I should think we'd be a bit scared, on top of that. Wouldn't we, Simon?'

'I should think so,' said Simon earnestly.

'Ah. It can't have been you then. My eyes aren't so good now, not without my glasses. Well, I think I'd better be getting along.' Mrs Verity waited for a moment for someone to say they didn't think she should, and, when nobody did, heaved herself to her feet and departed. They watched her back view disappearing down the lane.

Mrs Harrison said, 'There. Now I feel all nasty. I should have offered her a cup of tea. But I've got these letters to write sometime today and if I don't do them now I never will. James, have you touched my writing-pad? It was on the table.'

'No.'

'Oh for goodness sake! Things walk in this house—they really do. Oh, there it is under the dresser. How on earth did it get there? Could you get it for me, please?'

'Yes, Mum.' James, under the dresser, lingered, making faint scuffling noises. Mrs Harrison looked at him suspiciously.

'What are you doing, James? Don't tear pages off it.'

'The top one got rather dirty,' said James, emerging, red-faced. 'So I just tidied it up a bit. Here you are. I expect the wind blew it down there. Coming out, Simon? Bye, Mum. We'll just be in the orchard. Thanks for the cake-mix, Mum. Come on, Simon. Bye, Mum.'

Outside, he said, 'Phew!'

'What's up?' said Simon. 'What's that bit of paper?'

James held it out without a word. In Thos. Kempe's now familiar writing, in Mrs Harrison's fountain pen this time, was written

My goode ladye, I must tell thee that thy neighboure is a wytche. I have looked in the crystalle & I knowe it is shee hath caused your illnesse & furthermore it is well known that a wytche will call at the howse to inquire how is the illnesse that shee hath herselfe caused by her evill crafte, Thou must accuse her & bring her to justice. Make haste, or shee will doe more wickednesse.

Simon read it through. His glasses slipped down his nose, and were hunched up again.

'*Now* do you believe?' demanded James.

'Well,' said Simon cautiously, 'sort of. I mean I do because I don't see how it can be happening otherwise unless it's you playing an enormous joke on everyone me included ...'

James glared.

'... and I don't think you are actually because you wouldn't be getting yourself into trouble on purpose, would you?'

'No,' said James, 'I wouldn't.'

'But then the problem is me not really believing in ghosts. Because I've just never heard of this sort of thing ever happen-

49

ing to anyone before.' He gazed at James, amiable and slightly apologetic.

'It must be nice,' said James. 'Being so sure about what you believe in and what you don't.' He said it in a freezing voice, but Simon was not the kind of person who could be easily frozen. He grinned and began to climb the apple tree.

James followed him. He tore the note into very small pieces and stuffed it into a hole in the trunk.

'Nobody,' he said, 'absolutely nobody, not even Dad, is allowed to use Mum's best pen. It's the sort of thing that really makes her create. It would have been no pudding for about five years if she'd seen that.'

'No pudding for the sorcerer, then,' said Simon, chuckling.

James gave him a sour look. 'Huh. He doesn't exactly need pudding, does he?'

They climbed trees and jumped out of them until an instinct they both had about meals told them it must be about time for supper. Simon went home, and James went into the house, trying to analyse the various smells that drifted from the kitchen window, and decide what was being cooked. Hunger, he thought, was one of the nicest feelings, so long as you knew something would shortly be done about it. Of course, one was hungry all the time, really, in a quiet kind of way, but about three or four times a day it built up into enormous peaks, great urgent mountains of hunger, huge great towering cliffs ...

'Hands,' said Mrs Harrison. 'And face too if you're feeling energetic.'

'Yes, Mum.' He climbed the stairs, still thinking fondly about imminent food. Tim shot past him, coming from somewhere higher up, his ears laid back and his tail clamped between his hind legs. He looked rather as though someone had just kicked him, but that wasn't possible. Mr Harrison might not care for him particularly, but he never did more than pass remarks, and Helen wasn't cruel to animals. Only brothers, thought James, studying his fingernails abstractedly. If you grew them very long, and got them really splendidly dirty, and then planted little tiny seeds, would things grow in them? Maybe that was why people who are good at gardening are said to have green fingers. Like Aunt Mary. Next time she came to stay he must have a good look: perhaps really she had a fringe of minute seedlings growing at the ends of her fingers ...

Tim continued to behave oddly throughout the meal. To begin with he cowered under the table, making threatening noises in the back of his throat, and then once, when the door drifted open, and slammed itself shut again, he shot out snarling, took a large bite at the air midway between the door and sink, and bolted back under the table again.

'She was right, old Mrs V.,' said Mrs Harrison, shivering. 'We will have to get something done about these draughts. They seem to come even when the windows are tight shut. More, James?'

'Yes, please,' said James. 'Anything there is.' He was suspicious, and a little uneasy. The house had a faintly disturbed feeling, as though it was waiting for something to happen. Doors swung restlessly on their hinges, little currents of air fled past, lifting the edges of curtains and pushing Helen's hair across her face so that she had to keep wiping it back, crossly. Tim, under the table, peered out, growling.

'That dog's beginning to get on my nerves,' said Mr Harrison. 'It's unbalanced, if you ask me.'

'I say!' said Helen. 'There's a policeman stopping at the gate.'

The Harrisons stared out of the window. Sure enough, there was. Getting out of a small blue van, looking at something written on a pad in his hand, and checking it against the name on the gate.

James found that everybody was looking at him.

'I haven't done anything!' he said hotly.

'Forgive us,' said Mr Harrison. 'Unfair, I know. One shouldn't jump to conclusions. But there was that small episode last year, you must admit.'

Tim flew into the hall, barking, though it was not quite clear whether he had seen the van or not. He had, in any case, a fanatical dislike of policemen which seemed to hint at past dealings with them.

Mr Harrison put on his jacket and went out into the hall. Steps could be heard coming up the garden path. James got hold of Tim and held his mouth shut to keep him quiet: as he did so he had a curious sensation. A chunk of air beside him gathered itself together, became solid, and nudged him: a firm, cantankerous little shove.

There was a knock at the door. Mr Harrison opened it. The policeman was outside. He looked again at the piece of paper in his hand, then up at Mr Harrison, and said, 'Does Thomas Kempe live here?'

5

'No,' said Mr Harrison. 'Not here. You've been given the wrong address, I'm afraid.'

The policeman looked again at his piece of paper.

'East End Cottage?'

'Yes, that's right. But there's only us here. Myself, my wife, and two children.'

'No lodger? Relatives?'

'Absolutely none,' said Mr Harrison. 'Sorry.'

A gust of wind shook the front door, so that Mr Harrison had to hold on to it to prevent it slamming in the policeman's face. His uniform cap was blown off on to the path.

'You'd better come inside,' said Mrs Harrison.

'Thank you.' The policeman picked up his cap and stepped into the hall. Mr Harrison closed the door, which rattled violently as though someone tried to follow. The front garden was now lashing under a gale which flattened the long grass beside the path and bounced the late roses sprawling over the fence.

'Well, that's odd,' said the policeman.

'What did you want him for?' said Mrs Harrison. 'Or shouldn't one ask.'

'I don't see any harm, seeing he's not here anyway. It's about this business at the surgery. It got smashed up last night —I daresay you've heard. There was this note left on top of the

mess, kind of a signature, almost. Bit funny really.' He held
out the piece of paper. James craned his head under his father's
elbow to get a look at it.

'Yes,' said Mrs Harrison. 'Isn't that strange. "Thos. Kempe.
East End Cott." What peculiar writing. It reminds me of
something ...'

'Tombstones,' said Helen.

'Yes. Maybe. Perhaps there's some other East End Cottage?'

'No,' said the policeman. 'We made enquiries. Well, sorry
to have bothered you.'

'Not at all,' said Mr Harrison. 'Sorry we couldn't help.'

He was turning over the pages of the telephone directory.
'No Kempes here either, I see. Not in Ledsham.'

'Some joker ...' said the policeman gloomily. 'I daresay it
was the same lot as did the 'phone kiosks last week.' He
apologized once again for disturbing them, and departed. Tim
watched him go from behind a lavender bush and flew out

54

barking ferociously as soon as he was out of the gate, as though he would have made short work of him if only he'd seen him in time. The Harrisons settled down for the evening. And so, apparently, did Thomas Kempe: there were no more disturbances that night.

'It *was* him,' said James. He had met Simon on the corner and they were walking to school together.

'What was who?'

'The person who messed up the surgery. It was the sorcerer.'

'How do you know?'

'He left a note. With his name. And our address. A policeman came last night.'

'Did you tell the policeman what you think he is?' said Simon with interest.

'No.'

'Why not?'

'Because I'm fed up with nobody admitting he is one except me,' said James. 'That's why.'

He was too busy during the rest of the day to think much more about the problem. It was true about the measles: there were only about half the usual number of children in school, which was rather pleasant, creating a faintly holiday atmosphere, with the teachers amiable and indulgent, and unlimited helpings of dinner. James and Simon, who normally shared a table with two others, found themselves alone, able to spread out without knocking over inkpots or putting an elbow on someone else's exercise book. Mr Hollings, the headmaster, who taught their class, was in an experimental mood, full of new ideas about things for them to do. They did a new kind of sum which involved much measuring of the playground and generally rushing about with rulers and diagrams, and some more work on the Greek project, with some new books Mr Hollings had brought from the library for looking things up in, and finally they started on a relief map of Greece, nice and messy with flour and water. Indeed, they got so involved that they decided to stay in and get on with it at playtime instead of going outside.

They were bent over the board together, arguing about the construction of a mountain range.

'More,' said James. 'That's not high enough.'

'Yes it is. Because that lot ought to be higher, see?'

Mr Hollings came in, and began to shuffle through a heap of papers on his desk.

'Let's have the flour a minute,' said Simon.

All of a sudden James became aware, in the curious way that one often senses a shift in someone else's attention without looking at them, that Mr Hollings was staring hard at something. He looked up, and followed the direction of his stare, to the blackboard at the far end of the classroom.

Thomas Kempe's handwriting was spread boldly across the whole thing, obliterating a couple of sums and a list of words for spelling.

'Master Hollyngs' it said peremptorily, 'the sicknesse that is everywhere hath for certeine its cause in the worke of some wicked person : the Widdow Veritie is perhaps the guilty partie for shee is a wytche. Marke my words. I lyke not your wayes of teaching these childrene. They learn neither Latin nor Greeke & their manner of studie smacks too muche of playe. Thou would do well to beate them more.'

At the end was added, as an afterthought :
'James Harrison is my apprentice. He is idle & does not doe my bidding : I counsell thee to watche him.'

Mr Hollings crossed the room and read the message through, for a second time. James, speechless, had the odd sensation that he was actually frozen to his chair.

56

Then Mr Hollings laughed. 'I like the old-fashioned style, I must say,' he said. 'It's got a very authentic ring to it. Round about the seventeenth century, I'd say. Where did you get the idea, James?'

James felt himself reddening gradually and inevitably from the neck up. He looked at Simon for help, and Simon gazed back, friendly but detached.

'I ...' said James weakly. 'You see ...'

'The script is rather good, too,' Mr Hollings went on. 'Ornate in the right places. You've obviously been reading the memorial stones in the church. But there's a real Mrs Verity in the village, isn't there? A neighbour of yours, if I remember rightly.'

'Yes,' said James.

'In that case you shouldn't throw accusations like that around, even as a joke. You never know where it'll lead to. That's one of the nastier things about the past—the habit of accusing harmless old ladies of being witches.'

'I didn't,' said James in anguish. 'I don't think—I mean it wasn't ...'

'Oh, I'm sure you didn't mean any harm,' said Mr Hollings. A note of instruction crept into his voice as he went on, 'Why do you think people used to be so ready to believe in witchcraft?'

James said nothing. His voice seemed to have sunk, like a stone, down into his legs or feet or somewhere. He could see Simon looking at him, his eyes, behind the thick glass of his spectacles looking large and faintly wobbly like something seen through water. 'Not really,' said Simon helpfully. 'Why?'

'Well,' said Mr Hollings, 'I think the idea nowadays is that people were trying to find some explanation for all the unpleasant things that happen all the time in terms of magic and witchcraft. And of course for most people then things were pretty unpleasant most of the time.'

James hauled his voice up from somewhere a long way down and said, 'Oh. I see.'

Mr Hollings was warming to his subject. 'Of course,' he went on, 'there were so-called witches, who were mostly harmless old women, and then there were all the people who dabbled in astrology and alchemy and quack medicine and so forth. Wise men, they called themselves. Cunning men. Sorcerers.'

'Sorcerers?' said James.

'That's right. A different kettle of fish altogether. General meddlers. I daresay Ledsham was stiff with them. And no doubt they seemed to have their uses, too, in a world without doctors, or policemen, and with most people believing firmly in magic.' He began to rub the writing off the board. With a feeling of deep relief, James saw the rest of Thomas Kempe's message dissolve in a shower of chalk-dust.

'Nowadays we're more prepared to believe that things just happen,' said Mr Hollings with a flourish of the duster. 'We're not so sold on seeking explanations. Pick up those papers, would you, Simon, they keep blowing off the desk. And shut the window—there must be a draught. We just accept fate now, or whatever you like to call it. Maybe because our fates aren't usually so uncomfortable as our ancestors. I daresay if we'd been around in seventeenth-century Ledsham we'd have been clutching at mystical explanations for our misfortunes. If you're interested in this kind of thing you could do a little project on your own, James. What people's beliefs were in those days, eh?'

'Yes,' said James feebly. 'Yes. I could.'

Mercifully Mr Hollings was prevented from pursuing the matter by the inrush of people from the playground, as the bell went. The afternoon progressed without further reference to what had happened, except for one or two jokes by Mr Hollings, aimed in James' direction, about 'the sorcerer's

58

apprentice', which had James embarrassed and everyone else mystified.

On the way home, James brooded. At the corner of Swan Street he said, as much to himself as to Simon, 'He could have got me into dead trouble then. With Mr Hollings. It was just luck him taking it as a joke.'

'Yes,' said Simon.

James looked at him sharply. Twice, now, he'd seen Thomas Kempe in action. Twice. And still he wasn't convinced.

'You think I did it, don't you?'

'You *could* have ...'

'Well, I didn't.'

'No,' said Simon. 'I see.'

'You know something? You're as bad as people in his time —the sorcerer's time—like Mr Hollings was talking about. Just believing in things the way you think they are when they might be quite different.'

'Am I? Sorry.'

'Just because most people say there aren't such things as ghosts, you have to think like they do.'

'It's just that I don't feel sure.'

They walked on a bit. 'You would if you were me,' said James bitterly. 'You'd feel sure all right.'

'Everybody may not be like me,' said Simon. 'There may be ordinary people who believe in poltergeists and things. Ordinary grown-ups. Only they just don't talk about it. Your mum and dad might.'

This was a new, unexplored thought. James latched on to it, turned it over and over in his mind. There could very well be something in it. After all, A Clergyman had believed. Unshakeably and unquestioningly. By the time he reached home the idea had had time to develop and it began to seem to him that maybe he might have been mistaken all along. Perhaps he should have told his parents about Thomas Kempe right at the very beginning. He thought back to the scene of devastation in his bedroom, to their annoyance (to put it mildly) and his unresisting acceptance of the blame, not to mention the matter of the prescription and everything else. Perhaps he should have explained. Perhaps they would have accepted his explanation just like that. Perhaps he'd gone without all that pudding and forfeited all that pocket money for nothing. And, further, perhaps they knew how to deal with poltergeists. Maybe there was some quite simple, scientific, modern remedy that he just didn't happen to know about. Perhaps they were quite a common domestic problem, like blocked drains or mice, so ordinary that people didn't bother to mention them. He began to feel quite hopeful.

He decided to wait until the evening. If you have something important to say there is no point, he'd learned from experience, in saying it during the most active part of the day when people are coming home and getting meals and eating them and whatever you are trying to say gets lost in a commotion of doors opening and shutting and crockery banging and people asking where the newspaper is. He'd tested that out before now: he'd stood in the middle of the kitchen and said, 'I broke my leg at school today,' and his mother had turned the hot tap on and put another pile of plates in the sink and said, 'Yes, dear. I'll see about it tomorrow, dear.' No, it would be better to wait till later, when the household had subsided a little, come off the boil, so to speak, when his parents would be relaxed and more receptive.

Having spent an hour or so being helpful and unobtrusive, and especially friendly towards Helen, making tender enquiries about what sort of a day she'd had and so forth, so that she wouldn't be in a spiky, interrupting mood, he retreated to the apple tree, for a spell of rest and contemplation. He took the Personal Notebook with him, and began to fill it in; life must go on, no matter how large your problems may be. 'Pocket money,' he wrote. 'Situation as before. Emergency reserve now down to two lollies and one gob-stopper. Weather: Windy inside and out. Black beetles come out earlier now—is it because it gets dark earlier? Note: do scientific research on this. Could I put numbers on beetles with white paint?—no, cruel, I think. Will just have to watch carefully. Future plans: Find out more about poltergeists, if poss.' Here it occurred to him that such openness might be unwise. If Thomas Kempe could write, presumably he could read: James crossed out 'poltergeists' and wrote 'you-know-what.' 'Do other people have them and if so how do they get rid of them?' He changed his mind, crossed out 'get rid of them', and substituted 'get them altered'. This might be excessively cautious, but you didn't want him getting suspicious. He turned over the page and continued 'Excavate rubbish workmen threw out: let Simon join in maybe. Store apples somewhere in case I starve in the winter. Borrow biscuit from larder later and see if mice can be tamed. If so, train mice to carry messages. Find out if big chestnut tree in churchyard is climbable and if so climb it.' He closed the book, settled himself more comfortably in the fork of the tree, and abandoned himself to an enjoyable dream in which he became the first person to climb a hitherto undiscovered mountain thirty thousand feet above sea-level between Oxford and Burford. Simon came along to carry the oxygen equipment.

After dinner, when everyone had settled down, he raised the subject of poltergeists. He had thought out the presentation of what he was going to say very carefully.

'Dad?'

Mr Harrison turned over a page of the newspaper.

'Yes, James?'

James cleared his throat and began. 'What would you say,' he said, 'if a house suddenly began to behave in a very peculiar way. If things kind of moved without anyone moving

61

them and got mysteriously broken and books flew off book-shelves and bedcovers jumped off beds and doors banged them-selves. That kind of thing?'

'I'd say there was a boy around,' said Mrs Harrison crisply. 'Aged ten or so.'

James gave her a reproachful look.

'I can't imagine,' said Mr Harrison. 'Why do you ask?'

'You wouldn't think there might be a—well, some kind of ghost? A poltergeist, actually.'

'A *who*?' said Helen.

'Certainly not,' said Mr Harrison, lowering the newspaper. 'Since there aren't such things. I'd look for some rational explanation. If such a thing happened, which it wouldn't.'

'But if it had, and you were quite sure, and there wasn't any explanation?'

'Is something worrying you, dear?' said Mrs Harrison. 'You're not getting some silly idea in your head about this house, are you? Just because it's an old house.'

'But—there are books about poltergeists. So they must be true.'

'No, James,' said his father, folding the newspaper so that the crossword was neatly exposed, and looking round for a pencil. 'I'm afraid all such beliefs are just fantasies. Ghosts, poltergeists, the lot. They make a good story, that's all. And feed a peculiar appetite for the supernatural that some people have. But there's absolutely no scientific evidence for their existence at all: it's been proved time and again. They always turn out to have some simple explanation, or to be the product of someone's enlarged imagination. So get that idea out of your head.' He began to fill in the crossword, with precise, unhurried strokes of the pencil.

'Bed,' said Mrs Harrison. 'Both of you. And no more non-sense of that kind, James, or you'll be giving yourself night-mares.'

On the way upstairs Helen said, 'What on earth were you on about just then?'

'Nothing,' said James wearily. Commonsense, he realized, is as impenetrable as a stone wall.

6

Mr and Mrs Harrison were unusually irritable the next morning. They had had a very disturbed night, it seemed. The alarm clock, apparently, had kept going off at irregular intervals from midnight onwards.

'Why did it do that, Dad?' said James. He, too, had suffered: his bedcover had been twitched off three times, but there was no point in mentioning that.

'It's gone wrong, I presume,' said Mr Harrison, snappishly.

James said nothing: if people had to be so unswerving in their beliefs the only thing you could do was to let them go their own way.

The day passed uneventfully at school except for one or two more jokes about sorcery and sorcerer's apprentices from Mr Hollings, which James endured with resignation.

On the way home Simon said, 'Do they?'

'Do they what?'

'Believe in poltergeists.'

'No, they jolly well don't,' said James morosely.

'Oh,' said Simon. He picked up a stick from the gutter and began to run it along the wall of the row of cottages they were passing. The cottages were old: they must have stood square and solid in the middle of Ledsham for a very long time, maybe even since Thomas Kempe himself had stumped down this street, his head full of schemes and machinations about his neighbours and recipes for curing gout and palsy and the pox.

People had been going about their business past those walls year after year, different people in different times with different thoughts in their heads. Now, one small window displayed a notice saying that Walls Ice-cream was sold here, and on one of the front doors someone had chalked 'Arsenal for the Cup'. The chimney stacks bristled with television aerials.

'Nobody believes in him except me,' said James. 'And I wouldn't if I didn't have to.'

'Perhaps,' said Simon thoughtfully, 'he's only there for you.'

'What do you mean?'

'Perhaps he's a kind of personal ghost. I mean, maybe he's real all right but only for you.'

James considered this. It was possible.

'Well even if he is, the things he does are real for other people. Or he wouldn't be causing all this trouble, would he?'

'Maybe you should try talking to him again.'

'And have more encyclopaedias chucked at me?' said James. 'Thanks very much.'

They walked on in silence for a minute or two. There was a workman on the church tower, doing something to the stonework and carrying on a shouted conversation with a friend at the bottom about the seven-a-side match on Saturday afternoon.

'Trouble is,' said James, 'he's not in our time, is he? He's in his time, whenever that was, and he thinks like people thought in his time, and so you can't explain things to him in the same way we explain things to each other.'

'I should think he must be a bit bothered,' said Simon. 'It must be like waking up and discovering everyone except you has gone mad. Like a bad dream.'

'I'm not so sure he cares,' said James gloomily. 'I think he's just having a good time. I mean, nobody can do anything to him, can they? Since he's not even here properly. He can get away with anything.' Possibilities unfurled themselves, each more alarming than the last. The sorcerer could rampage un-

65

checked, while he, James, would be trapped in the ferment he left behind, held answerable for things he could not explain because no one would listen ...

'We've got to *do* something,' he said.

But Simon's attention had been distracted by the sight of unauthorized persons in the form of some boys from the other end of Ledsham throwing stones at the chestnut tree in *their* road. He vanished, leaving James with feelings of resentment: there was no doubt about it, Simon was only half-involved in the problem of Thomas Kempe. Interested, prepared to help up to a point, but not, like James, plunged into it day and night, like it or not.

He was still facing this fact, which made him feel isolated but, at the same time, challenged, like heroes of old confronted with impossibly difficult tasks, when he reached Mrs Verity's cottage. Mrs Verity was sitting on a chair in the doorway, enjoying the afternoon sunshine and keeping an eye on the various activities of East End Lane.

'Who'd like a mint humbug?'

'Yes, please,' said James.

'Let's see now, they were in my pinny pocket ... Here we are, dear. I've just seen your mother go past with her shopping so she'll be back now. There was one of those Bakery bags in her basket so I expect she's got something nice for your tea. There's nurse's car—I wonder where she's going?' Mrs Verity shifted her chair slightly to improve her view of the street. 'The telly repair van's still outside the Bradley's, I see. That's the best part of an hour he's been there.'

James stared up at Mrs Verity's thatched roof, admiring the patterned bit at the top and thinking that it must be very dull just being interested in what other people were up to. Starlings sat on the ridge of the roof, whistling and chattering. They gave the impression of doing much the same as Mrs Verity.

Mrs Verity was talking about school. She asked James how

he liked it and James said it was all right thanks and told her a bit about the project they were doing and Mrs Verity said 'Fancy!' and 'Dear me, it wasn't like that in my day.' And then rather surprisingly, she began to tell James a long story about a Sunday School when she was a small girl that began most unpromisingly and suddenly got very funny and unexpected. The Sunday School, it seemed, was a weekly session of torment during which all the Ledsham children of the time were made to sit in the cold and dusty silence of the church hall for two hours on end listening to the Scriptures read aloud, neither moving nor speaking on pain of instant and dreadful punishment. And on one never-to-be-forgotten occasion the children had slowly and delightedly become aware that the Vicar's dour sister who was responsible for inflicting this torture upon them was herself falling inexorably asleep . . .

'We all looked at each other and nobody hardly dared breathe and we waited till she dozed right off, sitting there in her chair with the Bible in her hand, and then my brother Robert—he was ever such a wicked boy, my brother, always in hot water, but he did well for himself later, manager of the Co-op. in Rugby he was till he retired—Robert signed to us all and we all got up, quiet as mice—not a sound, and we crept out and left her there and we turned the key in the lock behind us. And then we rushed out into the sunshine whooping and screeching like a lot of little savages and we played a wild game in the churchyard, in and out the gravestones. I can remember it now. Though it seems funny to think back—you hardly feel it could be the same person as you are now. But they say the child is father to the man, don't they?' She looked anxiously at James as though wondering whose father he might be and James stared back at her with a new interest. Somewhere, deep within stout, elderly Mrs Verity, with her rheumaticky hands that swelled up around her wedding ring, and her bad back that bothered her in damp weather, there sheltered

67

the memory of a little girl who had behaved outrageously in Sunday School. And that, when you stopped to think about it, was a very weird thing indeed.

He was just about to ask what happened when the Vicar's sister woke up when a tremendous gust of wind sent the starlings tumbling off the roofs—Mrs Verity's dress ballooned around her.

'Gracious! What a gale! I'll have to go inside.'

Air formed itself into a solid pressure on James' right arm, tugging him away from Mrs Verity's door. Another bank of it hustled him down the lane towards East End Cottage. Mrs Verity was controlling her skirts with one hand and pulling her chair into the house with the other.

'Goodbye for now, dear.'

James shouted 'Goodbye' as the wind gave him a final shove on to the opposite pavement and instantly subsided. Seething with indignation he ran the rest of the way home.

Bully. Busybody. Who does he think he is? I can talk to Mrs Verity if I want to, can't I?

Does he think he owns me, or something?

Mrs Verity had been right about the Bakery bag. There were cream splits for tea, which James found very heartening. After a while he felt sufficiently restored to tease Helen about her new dress.

'What's it s'posed to be? I never saw such a weird object. Oh, *I* know—it's a football jersey that someone left out in the rain so it got all soggy and stretched so it wasn't any use any more ...'

'It's a striped shift. Julia's got one too.'

'It's shifted all right. Shifted in all the wrong directions. Why's it such a peculiar shape—oh, *sorry*, that's you, I thought it was the dress ...'

'Mum!' wailed Helen.

'Enough!' said Mrs Harrison. 'And finish your tea, please. I want to clear up before the Vicar comes.'

'The *Vicar*?'

'About the choir.'

The Vicar, however, arrived before Mrs Harrison had had time to establish order in the kitchen. Moreover, he was one of those people who like to make it instantly clear that they are unusually accommodating and easygoing, and refused to be steered into the sitting-room.

'Please—I do hate people to put themselves out—just carry on as though I weren't here.'

That, thought James, would be a bit difficult. The Vicar was six feet tall and stout into the bargain. He had already clipped his head on a beam as he came in and was trying desperately to suppress a grimace of pain.

'Oh dear,' said Mrs Harrison, sweeping crockery into the sink. 'These blessed ceilings. I'm so sorry. Will you have a cup of tea? I'll just make some fresh.'

The front door slammed with a loud bang, making the Vicar jump. 'I never refuse a cup of tea—but please—I don't want to be a nuisance.'

'No trouble,' said Mrs Harrison. 'James, do something about that dog. It seems to have gone mad.'

Tim had gone into the now familiar routine that indicated, James realized with a sinking heart, that Thomas Kempe was not far away. He grabbed him. The Vicar, too, was looking at him, though apparently for different reasons.

'Dear me, how like the stray who got in and took the joint from our larder last week. Curious to see two mongrels so much alike, eh? Well, well. And how's school, young man?'

'Fine,' said James, 'thanks.' Tim was struggling violently, and lunging with bared teeth at a point somewhere behind the Vicar. The windows rattled. 'These autumn winds,' said the Vicar. 'I always think of those at sea.'

'What?' said Mrs Harrison. 'Oh, yes, yes, quite.' She slammed the lid on the teapot irritably.

The electric light flickered. Upstairs, distantly, came the sound of an alarm clock going off. A cup jinked in its saucer on the dresser.

'Do sit down,' said Mrs Harrison. 'James, pull up a chair for the Vicar.'

James fetched the windsor chair from the corner and placed it by the table. He still had one hand on its arm as the Vicar began to lower himself into it, and so felt the whole thing twitch, stagger, and jerk suddenly sideways, so that the Vicar, prodded violently in the hip, lurched against the table and almost fell.

'James!' said Mrs Harrison angrily. 'Look what you're doing!'

'Sorry,' said James in confusion, straightening the chair. The Vicar sat down, rubbing his hip and also apologizing. Tim began to bark hysterically.

'Put that dog out!' shouted Mrs Harrison.

With Tim outside, things were quieter, except for another bang as the back door, this time, slammed. The Vicar passed a hand across his forehead and rubbed his head, furtively.

'Family life, eh! There's always something going on, what?'

'Never a dull moment,' said Mrs Harrison grimly. 'Milk?'

'Oh—please—yes, if I may ... So kind of you. I do hope I'm not interrupting. I'm sure you're very busy, like we all are these days, eh?'

'Not at all,' said Mrs Harrison. 'James, pass the Vicar his tea, will you?'

James, with extreme caution, carried cup and saucer across the room. He was standing in front of the Vicar, and the Vicar's fingers were just closing on the edge of the saucer, when the cup jolted, tipped, hung at an angle of forty-five degrees, and turned over. Tea flowed into the saucer, and

71

thence in a cascade on to the Vicar's trousers.

'James!' said Mrs Harrison in a strangled voice.

There was a great deal of mopping and exclaiming. The Vicar apologized, and then apologized again. James apologized. Mrs Harrison's face had taken on that pinched, gathered look that foretold an outburst as soon as circumstances permitted. Finally, the Vicar, dried off and supplied with a new cup of tea, stopped saying how sorry he was and began to talk about choir practices. Mrs Harrison liked to sing sometimes: she said it allowed her to let off steam. Furthermore, she thought it would be a good idea if James sang. James, knowing this, had been hoping to beat a retreat. He sidled towards the door. 'My son,' said Mrs Harrison, glaring at him, 'sings too. After a fashion.'

'My dear boy,' said the Vicar, 'you must come along. We've got some other chaps about your age.'

James mumbled that he'd love to, or words to that effect. He was pinned to the spot now, by a steely look from his mother.

'Splendid, eh?' said the Vicar. 'Tell you what, I'll just jot down the times of our practices, shall I?' He patted his pockets.

Mrs Harrison said, 'James. Fetch the telephone pad, please, and a pencil.'

James opened the kitchen door, which swung shut again behind him, and crossed the hall. The telephone pad had a shopping list on it which said 'Onions, cereals, elastic bands, disinfectant.' Underneath that was a message about an electrician who would call back later, and a picture of a spaceman (drawn by James), and underneath that was a message from Thomas Kempe in large letters, which said 'I am watchynge ye.'

'Go on and watch then,' shouted James, in a fury. 'See if I care!'

There was a crash. The barometer had leapt off the wall and

lay on the floor, the glass cracked. And a series of loud bangs, apparently made by some kind of blunt instrument, such as a hammer, reverberated through the house.

The kitchen door flew open. The banging ceased instantly. Mrs Harrison was standing there saying the kind of things that were to be expected, only slightly toned down in deference to the Vicar, who was standing behind her, with a dazed expression on his face. He had hit his head on the beam again, James realized.

'... must apologize for my son's appalling behaviour,' concluded Mrs Harrison.

'Boys will be boys,' said the Vicar, without conviction. 'Eh? And now I really must be on my way. So kind ... So glad we can look forward to having you with us ... Do hope I haven't kept you from anything ...' He edged sideways through the front door, stooping, with the air of a man who wanted only to be unobtrusive and had always wished himself several sizes smaller.

James picked up the barometer and waited for the wrath to come.

Upstairs, later, James catalogued the extent of his mother's displeasure in the Personal Notebook. 'No pudding, obviously. Maybe I'll die of starvation, and *then* they'll be sorry. Bed straight after supper. Which is why I'm here. No Simon to play for two days.'

He turned over the page, and a new message confronted him, written with surly disregard across a whole clean page of the notebook.

I lyke not Priestes.

James tore it out, screwed it into a ball, and hurled it across the room.

For the rest of that evening, and the next day, James was

73

plagued by something which was lurking in the back of his mind, but which he could not quite pin down. In that book in the library, 'A Clergyman' had talked at great length not only about ghosts he had known, but also the disposing of ghosts. There had been a word which kept cropping up. Exercising them, or something like that. But how had it been done? And who by? He asked Simon. Simon could not remember either. Indeed it was difficult to involve him very deeply in the problem. He was, James realized, a little bitterly, an interested spectator. Sympathetic, helpful to a point, but sceptical and a spectator only.

There was no point in raising the matter with his parents again. They did not believe in ghosts: therefore there were no such things.

It occurred to him that this was a subject on which Mrs Verity might well have something to say. Naturally, he would not mention Thomas Kempe. That would be madness. It would be all over Ledsham in five minutes. And straight back to his parents, who would say he had made the whole thing up. No, the thing would be to raise the subject in a general sort of way, and see what happened ...

'Ghosts?' said Mrs Verity. 'Why, good gracious, I could tell you a thing or two about ghosts. Believe in them? Well, what I always say is, we don't know the answers to everything, do we? I mean, there's some things in this world you can't explain and maybe we're not meant to.'

It became clear that not only did Mrs Verity believe firmly in ghosts but she relished a good haunting, and knew about plenty. Ghost story followed ghost story in bewildering succession: what Mrs Verity's sister had seen in the churchyard after the Christmas Carol Service, what old Charlie at the Bull had heard in the yard one night, the story they used to tell about the Manor, in the old days. Ledsham apparently crawled with ghosts. In such abundance they rather lost their impact:

74

James began to grow restless. At last he managed to stem the flow and ask how you got rid of them.

'You have them exorcised, don't you, dear?' said Mrs Verity. 'By an exorcist. Excuse me just a moment—I can see Mrs Simpson just down the road and I've been wanting a word with her ...'

So he had, in a way, been right. Ghosts were a domestic problem, if not a particularly common one. And ordinary, ghost-believing people simply got someone in to deal with them like they'd get in a plumber or a window-cleaner. But he, of course, had to have parents who insisted on denying their existence even when living cheek by jowl, so to speak, with a particularly active one.

If you need a plumber, or anything in that line, you look in the Yellow Pages of the Telephone Directory, don't you? Right, then. James looked, not entirely hopefully. As he had expected, there were no exorcists. Nothing between Exhibition Stand Contractors and Export Agents. There was nothing for it but to consult Mrs Verity again. Cautiously, though, in case her interest was aroused.

'Do I know any exorcists? Well, let me see now ... There's Mrs Nash, but she's really more in the fortune-telling and teacup line. I don't think she's ever done much in the spiritual way. Of course sometimes you find the Vicar'll turn his hand to that kind of thing, but not this one, I'm told. Now, when they had that trouble at Church Hanborough, years ago, at that old place there, they called in Bert Ellison. Mind, he's a wart-charmer really. And water-divining he does, too, they say. Why do you ask, dear?'

James did not dare pursue the matter too far. He returned to the Yellow Pages, and found that Wart-charmers and Water-Diviners are not included either. There was, however, a Bert Ellison, Builder, who lived in one of the cottages behind the church.

The thought of confronting this person all on his own, and stating his business, threw James into confusion. He imagined what might happen: 'Will I come and get rid of a ghost for you? I'm a builder, aren't I? Says so, doesn't it? Bert Ellison, builder. I wouldn't like to think you might be trying to make a fool of me ...'

A particularly restless evening, however, during which Thomas Kempe fused the television set and broke a milk jug, stiffened his resolve. The next day, after school, he walked round to the lane behind the church.

There was a small blue notice-board attached to the wall of Bert Ellison's cottage. It said only that he was a Builder and Decorator, and gave Free Estimates, without mentioning his other activities, which was discouraging but perhaps only to be expected. James knocked at the door.

The man who opened it wore a dusty boiler-suit and had a mug of tea in one hand. He was heavily-built, and slightly balding. 'Yes?' he said.

James said, 'Mr Ellison?'

'That's me.'

'I've come about a—well, a job that needs doing.'

'Decorating, is it?' said Bert Ellison, taking a gulp of tea.

'No, no, it isn't, actually.'

'Building, then?'

'No,' said James. 'Not that either.'

Bert Ellison looked at him reflectively. 'I don't know you, do I? Come from your mum, have you? What's her name, then?'

'I'm James Harrison. We live at East End Cottage. Actually it's for me, the job, not for my mum.'

'Is it, now? Well, I'm blowed. Bit young, aren't you, to be handing out jobs?'

'It's just a small job,' said James unhappily. 'At least I hope it is.'

'I think you'd better come in,' said Bert Ellison, 'and tell me about this job of yours. Mind, I'm not saying as I can fix you up. We'll have to see.'

'Thank you very much, Mr Ellison,' said James.

'You'd better call me Bert, if we're going to do business together.'

Bert was clearly not married. The kitchen was full of empty milk bottles and socks drying on a line over the stove. Tins of paint and brushes littered the table, along with the remains of some fish and chips in newspaper and a large brown teapot.

'Now then?'

James decided to plunge straight in. 'There's a ghost in our house,' he said, 'and I thought—at least somebody told me— maybe you could do something about it.'

Bert poured himself another cup of tea, and began to roll a cigarette. He stuck it in the corner of his mouth, lit it, and said, 'Just the one?'

'Yes,' said James, taken aback.

'It's as well to ask. I've known them come in pairs. Or more. Been there long, has it?'

'About a week or so. Or at least I've only known about it that long.'

'Could have been dormant,' said Bert, 'and something sparked it off, like. Why've you come about it, and not your mum?'

'She doesn't believe in them. Nor does my dad.'

'Ah. You find people like that from time to time. No point in arguing with 'em. It's best just to get on with the job, I always say. They'll thank you for it in the long run. Now, what's he been up to, this bloke?'

James described the sorcerer's activities in detail. Bert Ellison listened intently, drinking his tea and smoking. When James had finished he passed a large hand across his chin once or twice, and stared out of the window.

'You've got a problem there, all right,' he said. 'I never come across one quite like that before. The knocking, yes, and the breaking things, and all that. It's the notes is unusual. I never came across one as could write up to now.'

'He must've lived there,' said James, 'hundreds of years ago.'

'That's right. They're often the worst to get rid of, too. They feel at home. Stands to reason, doesn't it?'

'Can't you do anything, then?'

'I'll have a go, but I can't promise too much, mind. Still, I daresay I can fix you up. There's a charge, of course.'

'I've only got forty pence at the moment,' said James. 'I've been having a bit of trouble about pocket money lately.'

'We'll say five bob, shall we,' said Bert. 'I do a reduced rate for pensioners, too.'

'Thank you very much.'

'How about I look in tomorrow evening?'

'The thing is,' said James, 'I don't know what to say to my mum about you.'

'Ah. Now you've got a point there. Being as how she's a non-believer, as you might say. She's not seen these notes, then?'

'No. And if I showed her she'd just say I'd written them.'

'Ah. Fair enough. What's she done about this clock, then, and the telly packing up?'

'She took the clock to the shop in the High Street, and the electrician's coming tomorrow.'

Bert snorted contemptuously. 'If you've got dry rot in the floorboards, you don't just slap new lino down on top, do you? That won't do her much good. Still, if that's the way she feels about it there's not much use you going home and saying "Look mum, I got a bloke coming in tomorrow to see about the ghost", is there?'

'No,' said James.

Bert tapped blunt, competent-looking fingers on the table-

78

top for a moment. Then he said, 'Got any building jobs need doing?'

'Well ...' said James. 'It was all done before we moved in, really. The catch on my window's broken, though. She did say she'd get that done some time. Oh, and they did say I needed some shelves, too.'

'There you are, then. Now what you've got to do is, go home and start in on them about that and when they say "Well, yes, but who's going to do it?" you chip in smart and say you've heard about this Bert Ellison as everyone speaks so highly of and how you'll nip along and ask him yourself ...'

'Yes!' said James excitedly. 'Yes, I could do that.'

'... and then I come round and fix your shelves and see to the window and while I'm there I'll have a think about the other business as well. How about that?'

'Great!' said James. 'Thanks very much.'

'So you look in on your way home from school, eh? And if everything's in order I'll be round later in the evening.'

7

'Bert Ellison?' said Mrs Harrison. 'I've never heard of him.'

'He's really a very well-known builder,' said James earnestly. 'Quite famous, actually. I'm surprised you don't know about him. I'm sure he'd do the shelves much better than anyone else.'

Mr Harrison, who had listened without saying anything, got up and began to put his coat on.

'At this point,' he said, 'one's bound to ask oneself certain questions. One: why, all of a sudden, does James want something urgently done in the way of mending a window and putting up some shelves that he's shown little or no interest in hitherto? And two: given all this, why does he go still further and produce a particular builder that he wants to do the job? One is tempted even to suspect some sort of conspiracy between the two of them ...'

'Dad!' said James, in the most shocked and offended voice he could manage.

'... if it weren't quite beyond belief that a perfectly sane, adult chap such as Bert Ellison should associate himself in any way with some lunatic scheme of James'.'

'Why? Do you know him?' said Mrs Harrison.

'Slightly. Or at least I know of him. He's been doing some work in the church. He seems quite all right. I should think we might entrust the shelves to him. James' sudden involvement will no doubt be one of those things that we shall never get to the bottom of. Like many others. Eh, James?'

'It's no good looking as though you don't know what he means,' said Helen. 'What about my dressing-gown cord being found tied to the big apple tree? And the empty ink-bottles in the vegetable patch ...?'

James sighed: there is nothing more boring than trying to explain things to people who aren't going to appreciate what it is you are up to. You've got to use something to haul provisions up a rock-face with, haven't you? And if you do scientific experiments you're bound to leave a few bits and pieces around, aren't you? (No point in telling Helen lettuces do not grow blue if watered with diluted ink: she wouldn't even care).

'So can I say it's all right if he comes tonight?' he said, ignoring Helen.

'I suppose so.'

Bert Ellison arrived on a bicycle shortly after tea, whistling. He looked so ordinary, so, in fact, like a builder on his way to put up some shelves that for a moment James' faith was shaken. Only ten minutes before he had enjoyed saying to Simon, 'Well, I'm afraid I'll have to go now because I've got this exorcist coming in to see to the poltergeist.' Simon had been satisfactorily astonished. But now here was Bert, in white overalls, with a cigarette tucked behind his ear, and a black bag of tools, not looking in the least like an exorcist.

'Oh,' said Mrs Harrison. 'Yes, of course, the window, and the shelves ... I'd better take you up.'

James, lurking behind her in the hall, fidgeted anxiously, and saw Bert's gaze come up over her shoulder and fall on him. The man pushed his cap back from his forehead, unhitched the cigarette from his ear and said, 'Maybe your young lad could do that. Not to bother you, see?' James was filled with relief.

Mrs Harrison said, 'Well, yes, you could, couldn't you, James?' and went back into the kitchen. James looked at Bert Ellison, and Bert Ellison nodded, and they went upstairs, James leading and Bert following, his heavy tread making the whole staircase sway slightly.

James opened the door to his room and they went in. Tim, asleep on the bed, woke up with a start and growled.

Bert looked at him thoughtfully. 'I seen him before,' he said. 'Let's think now ... At the butcher's before Christmas, and The Red Lion before that, and the corner shop the year before that. He knows when he's on to a good thing, that one.' Tim, with an evil look, slunk past him and out of the door. Bert set his tools down with a clatter and surveyed the room. 'Right, then, where are we putting these shelves?'

'But,' began James anxiously, 'the other thing ...'

'Look,' said Bert, 'we've got to be doing something, haven't we? If your mum decides to come up. Not larking about looking for ghosts. These shelves has got to go up, and be heard to go up.'

James understood. 'Here,' he said. 'Under the window.'

Bert began to measure, and cut pieces of wood. 'So he played up when the Vicar was here, this bloke?'

'I'll say,' said James. 'It was one of the worst times. Knocked things over, and banged.'

'Then it's not worth trying bell, book and candle,' said Bert, 'if he's got no respect for the Church. I'd just be wasting my time. Nor's it worth getting twelve of them.'

'Twelve what?'

'Vicars,' said Bert briefly.

James had a delightful, momentary vision of twelve enormous Vicars following one another up the stairs, hitting their heads on the beams and apologizing in chorus. But Bert was not just being fanciful. He was not a man given to fancy. Apparently ghosts were normally exorcised by twelve priests

82

in the old days. Or seven, sometimes. Or just one, if skilled in such matters.

'But that won't do with this blighter,' said Bert. He lit the cigarette from behind his ear, made some token noises with hammer and nails, and looked round the room reflectively. James waited for him to come to a decision, anxious, but at the same time deeply thankful to be thus sharing the burden of responsibility for Thomas Kempe. He felt relieved of a heavy weight, or at least partly relieved.

'No,' said Bert. 'We won't try anything like that. Nor talking to him, neither, since you say you've already had a go. You know what I think? I think we'll try bottling him.' He put a plank of wood across the chair, knelt on it, and began to saw it in half, whistling through his teeth.

'Bottling him?' said James, wondering if he could have heard correctly.

'That's right. I'll be wanting a bottle with a good firm stopper. Cork 'ud be best. And seven candles.'

'Now?'

'Might as well get on with it, mightn't we?'

James raced downstairs. On the landing he slowed up, remembering the need for discretion. He crept down the next flight, and tiptoed into the larder. He could hear his mother and Helen talking in the kitchen, and from overhead came reassuringly ordinary sawing and hammering noises made by Bert. He felt nervous on several counts: there was the problem of someone asking him what he wanted, and also he kept expecting the sorcerer to manifest himself in some way. What was he doing? Could he be scared of Bert Ellison? Or was he biding his time, before launching some furious counter-attack? From what Thomas Kempe had revealed of his character hitherto he didn't seem the kind of person to be all that easily routed, even by as phlegmatic an opponent as Bert Ellison.

There were various empty medicine bottles on the larder

shelf. He selected the one with the tightest-fitting cork and began to look for candles. There was a box of gaily coloured birthday-cake ones, complete with rose-shaped holders, but they seemed inappropriate. He hunted round and unearthed a packet of uncompromisingly plain white ones—an emergency supply for electricity cuts. They were just right: serviceable and not frivolous. He was just putting them under his arm when the door opened.

'Mum says if you're picking at the plum tart you're not to,' said Helen. 'What *are* you doing with those candles?'

'The builder needs them,' said James. 'He's got to solder the shelves with something, hasn't he? He can't solder the rivets without a candle, can he? Or the sprockets.' He stared at her icily: Helen's ignorance of carpentry was total, he knew.

She looked at the candles suspiciously. 'I don't see ...' she began.

'You wouldn't,' said James, wriggling past her. 'I should go and ask Mum to explain. Very slowly and carefully so you'll be able to follow her all right. Or if you like I will later on.' He shot up the stairs without waiting to hear what she had to say.

Bert had cleared the table and moved it to the centre of the room.

'Ah,' he said, 'that'll do fine. We'll have it in the middle, the bottle, and the candles in a circle round, like. He seems to be keeping himself to himself, your chap. I thought we'd have heard something from him by now.'

'So did I,' said James.

'Maybe he's lying low to see what we've got in mind. Is that his pipe on the shelf there?'

'Yes.'

Bert walked over and picked it up. As he did so the window slammed shut.

'There. He don't like having his property interfered with. Well, that signifies.'

'Can we get on,' said James uneasily, 'with whatever we're going to do.'

'No good rushing a thing like this,' said Bert. 'You've got to take your time. Make a good job of it.' He fiddled around with the bottle and candles, arranging them to his liking. Then he struck a match and lit the candles. The flames staggered and twitched for a moment, then settled down into steady, oval points of light.

'We'd best draw the curtains,' said Bert. 'We don't want people looking in from outside. Then pull up a chair and sit down.'

With the curtains drawn, the room was half dark, the corners lost in gloom, everything concentrated on the circle of yellow lights on the table. Bert and James sat opposite one another. The candles made craggy black shadows on Bert's face, so that it seemed different: older, less ordinary. Downstairs, a long way away, the wireless was playing and someone was running a tap.

Bert took out a handkerchief and wiped his forehead. 'Right, then.' He cleared his throat and said ponderously, 'Rest, thou unquiet spirit!'

There was dead silence. Bert, catching James' eye, looked away in embarrassment and said, 'I don't hold with thee-ing and thou-ing, as a rule, but when you're dealing with a bloke like this—well, I daresay he'd expect it.'

James nodded. They sat quite still. Nothing happened.

'Return from whence thou come—came,' said Bert. 'Begone!'

Two of the candles on James' side of the table guttered wildly, and went out.

'Ah!' said Bert. 'Now he's paying us a bit of attention.'

They waited. James could hear his mother's voice, distantly,

85

saying something about potatoes from the sack in the shed.
Uneasy, he leaned across towards Bert and whispered, 'Will it
take long?'

'Depends,' said Bert. 'It's no good chivvying these characters.
You've got to let them take their time.'

A draught whisked round the table. Three more candles
went out.

'Cheeky so-and-so, isn't he?' said Bert.

'Does he know what he's supposed to do?' whispered James.

'He knows all right.'

But how would *they* realize it if and when Thomas Kempe
did decide to conform and get into the bottle, James wondered?
He wanted to ask, but felt that perhaps too much talk was

unsuitable. Presumably Bert, as an experienced exorcist, would just know in some mysterious way.

'Come on, now,' said Bert. 'Let's be 'aving you.'

The last two candle-flames reached up, long and thin, then contracted into tiny points, went intensely blue, and vanished.

'That's it!' said Bert. He got up and drew the curtains.

James looked round anxiously. 'Didn't it work?'

'No. He wasn't having any. When the candles go out, that's it.'

'Couldn't we try again?'

'There wouldn't be any point to it. If he don't fancy it, then he don't fancy it, and that's that. He's an awkward cuss, no doubt about it.'

The stairs creaked. James whipped the candles off the table and into his drawer. Bert hastily began to saw up a piece of wood.

Mrs Harrison came in. 'Everything all right?' she said. 'You mustn't let James get in your way, Mr Ellison. I'm afraid he hangs around rather, sometimes.'

'That's all right,' said Bert, 'I'm not fussed. I can send him packing when I've had enough.'

'Good. What a funny smell. Wax, or something.'

'That'll be my matches,' said Bert, 'I daresay.'

Mrs Harrison said, 'Candles, I'd have thought.' She looked round, sniffing.

'Not to my way of thinking,' said Bert. 'That's a match smell, that is.'

'Oh. Well, maybe.' She gave Bert a look tinged with misgiving and looked at the pile of half-sawn wood: the thought seemed to be passing through her mind that not much had been achieved so far.

'I got behind,' said Bert amiably. 'We've been having a bit of a chat, me and your lad here. Found we had one or two interests in common, as you might say.'

'Oh?' said Mrs Harrison.

'History. People that aren't around any more. We've both got a fancy for that kind of thing.' Bert's right eyelid dropped in a conspicuous wink, aimed towards James.

'That's nice,' said Mrs Harrison. 'We hadn't realized James was particularly interested in history, I must say.'

'It's often their own parents as knows children least, isn't it?' said Bert.

'I'm not entirely sure about that,' said Mrs Harrison drily. James, avoiding her eye, busied himself with a pile of nails.

'So, one way and another I think I'll have to come back tomorrow and finish off,' said Bert, stowing hammer and saw into his black bag. 'I like to make a proper job of anything I take on. See it through to the end.'

Mrs Harrison said, 'Right you are, then,' and went downstairs. James and Bert Ellison, left alone, looked at each other.

'No,' said Bert, 'I can see she wouldn't have much time for ghosts, your mum. A bit set in her ways, maybe. Got opinions.'

'Yes,' said James with feeling. 'She has.'

'Not that I've got anything against that. I like a woman to know her own mind. But it's no good setting yourself up against it. You'd just be wasting your breath.' He pushed his ruler and pencil into the pocket of his white overalls, closed the tool-bag, and stood up.

James said anxiously, 'What about tomorrow? Is there something else you can try?'

'To be honest with you,' said Bert, 'there's not a lot. Vicars is out. He don't fancy the bottle.' His large stubby fingers came down on his palm, ticking off possibilities. 'We could try fixing him with a job as would keep him busy, but I'd guess he's too fly to be taken in with that one. Or we could try circle and rowan stick. Is your father an Oxford man, by any chance?'

'An Oxford man?'

'Did he go to Oxford University?'

'No,' said James. 'Why?'

'In the old days you used an Oxford man for laying a ghost. But I daresay there's not many would take it on nowadays. They've got fancy ideas in education now, I hear.'

'Isn't there anything then?' said James disconsolately.

'It's a tricky job, this one, no doubt about that.'

'You see I'm getting blamed for everything he does. It's no pocket money, and no pudding, and worse, I should think, when they run out of punishments.'

'That's a bit thick,' said Bert.

'I'll say.'

'The trouble is, them being non-believers. In the normal way of things it'd be them as would have called me in, in the first place. Things would have been a lot more straightforward.'

They were going down the stairs now. James glanced anxiously at the closed kitchen door. Bert nodded and lowered his voice. 'Tell you what, I got those shelves to finish off, so I'll be back tomorrow.'

'Thank you very much,' said James. 'Oh, I nearly forgot ...' He reached into his jeans pocket for his money.

'No charge,' said Bert. 'Not till the job's done satisfactory.' He climbed on to his bike and rode away down the lane, the black bag bumping against the mudguard.

James had been right in thinking that the sorcerer might be biding his time. That evening, as though in compensation for the restraint he had shown during Bert Ellison's visit (if it had been restraint, and not, perhaps, a temporary retreat in face of a professional enemy) he let rip. Doors slammed, and the house echoed with thumps and bumps, almost invariably coming from whatever area James was currently occupying, so that cries of 'James! Stop that appalling noise!' rang up and down the stairs. The television set, just repaired, developed a

89

new fault: a high-pitched buzzing that coincided oddly with all weather-forecasts and any programme involving policemen or doctors (which seemed to be most of them). The teapot parted from its handle when Mrs Harrison lifted it up, with catastrophic results. Something caused Tim, sleeping peacefully under the kitchen table, to shoot out yelping as though propelled by someone's foot, colliding with, and tripping up, Mr Harrison, who fell against the dustbin which overturned, shooting tea-leaves and eggshells across the floor ... You could put whatever interpretation you liked on all this: coincidence, carelessness, the weather, the malevolence of fate. James knew quite well to what he would attribute it, and so, apparently did Tim, who abandoned his usual evening sleeping-places and went to sulk in the long grass at the end of the orchard.

After a couple of hours Mr and Mrs Harrison, both remarkably even-tempered people in the normal way of things, were reduced to a state of simmering irritation, which eventually resulted in both James and Helen being sent to bed early and, they felt, unloved. They shared their resentment on the stairs.

'It's not fair,' said Helen.

'It's not *our* fault.'

'Everything keeps going wrong these days. I think it's something to do with this house.'

James stared. Such perception was unlike Helen: she seemed usually to notice only the obvious. Perhaps she was changing. Since they seemed to have established a temporary truce, he decided to investigate further.

'Helen?'

'Mmn.'

'Do you believe in ghosts?'

Helen said cautiously, 'Do you?'

'Well. I s'pose so. Yes, actually I do.'

'So do I, really.'

They looked at each other.

'*They* don't,' said Helen. 'Mum and Dad.'

'I know. But lots of people do.'

'Why do you want to know anyway? I say, you don't think there's one in this house, do you?'

James hesitated, tempted to confide. But you never knew with Helen ... She might well laugh, tell everyone, never let him hear the end of it. And he'd have to share Bert Ellison.

'Shouldn't think so,' he said, turning away. 'Good night.'

'Good night.'

He climbed the last few stairs to his room slowly, thinking of what he might have said to her. 'Yes, as a matter of fact there is. He's called Thomas Kempe, Esq., and he lived here a few hundred years ago and was a kind of sorcerer and crazy doctor and village policeman and general busybody and he thinks he's come back to start all over again with me helping and he keeps writing me messages and as a matter of fact I've been sharing my bedroom with him for over a week now.' Ha ha!

He opened the door. The bottle he and Bert Ellison had used in the exorcism attempt was in the middle of the floor, smashed. Beside it was Thomas Kempe's latest message, written in felt pen on the back of an envelope.

Doe not thinke that I am so dull of witte that I may be thus trycked twyce.

8 ———————————————————

Twice?

Not 'You're not going to trick me like that,' but 'You're not going to trick me like that *twice*.'

In other words, someone had tried to exorcise Thomas Kempe before. And, moreover, had succeeded.

When?

And how, or why, had he become un-exorcised?

Excited and preoccupied, James could think of nothing else all the next day. The thought that he was not the only person to have suffered from the sorcerer's attentions was in some way comforting, and even more comforting was the idea that this other person, whoever he might be, had been able to deal with him. If Thomas Kempe had been defeated once, then surely he could be defeated again?

'What's up?' said Simon, at school. 'You're half asleep.'

'No, I'm not. I'm just thinking.'

'Did this exorcist person come?'

'Mmn.'

'Well, what happened, then?'

'Nothing. It didn't work.'

'You mean he didn't really know how to?'

'No,' said James impatiently. 'What he tried to do didn't work because the sorcerer wouldn't have anything to do with it. He's going to have another go tonight.'

'Can I come and see?'

'No,' said James. Having gone to all the trouble of finding Bert Ellison he didn't feel disposed to share him with Simon, either. Besides, an exorcism wasn't exactly a public exhibition, was it? Maybe too many people around would spoil things. And on top of that he was disappointed in Simon. He hadn't really been as helpful as he might have been. He'd shown a proper interest, at least just lately he had, but when it came to actually *doing* anything, James had been on his own. So that now things were getting interesting, he'd stay on his own, he decided. They parted a little coolly after school.

Walking home, he tried to piece things together in his mind. The cottage, he knew, had been empty for some years before the Harrisons had bought it. Before that, he remembered hearing his mother say, it had been lived in by an elderly couple. It had been in a very bad state: a lot of repairs and so forth had been done before the Harrisons moved in. His room, he seemed to remember, had been in a particularly bad way. 'We even had to break the door down, and the floor was inches deep in dust.' Hadn't his mother said something like that? 'Nobody'd used it for goodness knows how long ...'

Suppose Thomas Kempe's return had been in some way connected with that? Suppose opening the room up again had released him somehow? But how, and why, had this other person got rid of him, and when? It began to seem very important to find out about all this. Important not just because it would be interesting but important because to know might, somehow, help with the problem of getting rid of him again.

It was Tim disappearing round the side of the cottage caked with the most astonishing amount of dried mud that gave James an idea. Tim had been digging, clearly, and the thought of digging reminded James of the mound of rubbish at the far end of the orchard that had been thrown out by the workmen when they were clearing out the cottage. Much of it was rubble, but there were other things as well—the carcases of old chairs, bundles of newspapers, boxes of junk, broken bits and pieces of various useless objects. Mr Harrison had been saying for sometime that he must ask the County Council to come and take it away.

You never knew: there might be a clue there.

James fetched a shovel from the coal-cellar and summoned Tim. He could make himself useful for once.

They excavated the south side of the heap without finding anything of interest, except a field-mouse's nest in a tuft of grass growing up between some bricks. There were five babies, barely as large as a thumb-nail, shrimp-pink, blind and throbbing, perfect in every detail. James, knowing it probable that Tim would eat them, reconstructed the nest and built a safer screen of bricks around it, leaving access tunnels for the mother mouse. Tim watched resentfully. Having done that, James switched to the other side of the mound and removed the outer wall of rubble. This was a little more promising: the skeleton of an old pram confronted him, with various things stuffed into its body: damp and yellowing newspapers, a tin hat, some rusty tools. He pulled out a pile of newspapers, and read the headlines: BREAD RATIONING TO CONTINUE, RUSSIA SAYS NO AGAIN. The dates were all a very long time ago. He heaved the whole pram out and revealed a central core of decomposing cardboard boxes. They were green with mould and Tim, burrowing excitedly among them, was clearly of the opinion that they had been the home of rats. James began to pull them out.

The first one was full of old clothes, congealed by damp and age into a brownish-black lump of cloth, its component parts barely identifiable. James pulled it apart, and found trousers, a jacket, something that might have once been a velvet hat, and other strange garments whose use was difficult to determine. They were all very old-fashioned. The next box was full of picture postcards, bundles and bundles of them, pictures of seascapes and landscapes in muddy brown colours, and kittens and vases of flowers and simpering girls in very covered-up bathing-dresses. It was becoming apparent that whoever had lived in the cottage and owned all this had never, ever, thrown anything away.

More boxes, more clothes, a batch of newspaper clippings dated 1919, all about aeroplanes (somebody must have been an early aviation enthusiast), more postcards, with some of the postmarks giving dates that began with 18 something instead of 19 something. James had the impression that the further he investigated, the further he was going back in time. There were some bundles of letters, too, tied up with grubby white tape: James undid one and the letters spilled on to his lap, all written in large sloping handwriting. He picked one up and read 'My dear Sister, Arnold is so very pleased to receive your kind invitation ...' He stopped, with a feeling of intrusion: you cannot read other people's letters, even if found in a rubbish heap. But then, catching sight of the date at the top of the letter, May 14th 1856, he realized with a jolt that the writer must have been dead for many, many years. Even so, he felt faintly uncomfortable, reading on '... he is a high-spirited boy, but of a pleasant disposition I do believe, even though a Mother must be prejudiced in such matters ...' The writing was hard to decipher, and full of long, loopy words. He put the letter back in the bundle and tied it up again.

He was just about to put the box with the letters in it to one side when he realized there was something else in it, right at the bottom. A small, leather-bound book. At first he thought it was a Bible, but then, opening it, found it full of handwriting, similar to, though not the same as, the handwriting in the letters. It was a diary. He turned over the pages, reading passages here and there, about going to church, and the weather being most agreeable, and the apples promising a

95

fine crop this year. Feeling uncomfortable again, for to read someone's diary, even someone long since dead, seemed even more prying than to read their letters, he was about to close it when two words in the spidery writing detached themselves from the rest and seemed to hit him smack between the eyes.

Thomas Kempe.

He blinked, and almost dropped the diary in his excitement. Pushing everything else aside, he sat down on one of the heaps of old clothes, and stared intently at the page. He started at the top and read '... the house has been set in quite an uproar by the creature, with doors and windows banging, china smashed, and such fearful high winds about that I have been driven half out of my mind. But the *worst* thing of all is that to begin with I thought poor Arnold responsible, and was quite vexed with the boy, telling the *poor* lad he must consider his aunt's advancing years and restrain his natural boisterousness. And now it turns out the turmoil is caused by a *ghost*, or rather I understand a *poltergeist*, which is a thing that exhibits itself by noise alone. Poor dear Arnold indeed has been most plagued of all by the thing for it devotes itself largely to him and writes him *messages* instructing him to do this and that, as though he were some kind of servant to it. Though I should say "he" not "it" for it appears from these messages that we are visited by the spirit of a certain Thomas Kempe, a sorcerer or cunning man who lived once in the house, in the time of King James I, I think. Truly, we are quite driven out of our wits ...'

There was a swishing noise: someone coming through the long grass. James shoved the diary quickly into the front of his shirt.

'What *are* you doing?' said Helen. 'Mum says you're to come in for tea.'

'All right.'

'You're filthy dirty, you know. What is all this stuff any-way?'

'Just things the workmen chucked out.'

'You shouldn't mess about with it,' said Helen, with distaste. 'You don't know what there mightn't be in there.'

You don't indeed, thought James, following her back through the orchard. You certainly jolly well don't. The diary was digging into him, tantalizingly. He itched to read more. Who was Arnold? How? Why? When?

He ate as little tea as he could without arousing suspicion, in the shortest time possible, and fled upstairs to his room. Then he flung himself down on the bed and began to read the diary from cover to cover.

It was dated 1856. It was the diary of a Miss Fanny Spence, who, it became apparent as he read on, was a middle-aged spinster lady. She lived quietly and alone in East End Cottage, going to church on Sundays, making preserves, busying herself with various charitable undertakings, writing to her relatives, indulging in small artistic endeavours with sea-shells and dried grasses. She did little that was of great interest, but her diary revealed her as a pleasant, friendly, humorous lady. Then, in May, she decided that it would be a good idea to invite her nephew, Arnold Luckett, aged ten, to spend the summer holidays with her (Of course, James thought, the letter—My dear Sister, Arnold is so very pleased ...) 'London is *not* an agreeable place for a child,' said the diary. 'The boy will be far better off in Ledsham if dear Mary will allow me to have him. I do hope he will not find an elderly aunt too tedious a companion. For my part I am in quite a fluster of excitement at the thought of a young person in the house.'

Aunt Fanny immersed herself in the business of preparing for Arnold's visit. She scurried round her friends and acquaint-ances, collecting recipes of delicious meals for the feeding of Arnold, she went to Oxford to buy him a fishing-rod ('I know that boys love to fish, and we have the Evenlode nearly on our doorstep: indeed I'm of a mind to try my hand myself'), she allowed herself to be carried away with enthusiasm and acquired a puppy from the farm down the road, and finally she decided that the spare bedroom would not do, but that she must have the old attic room done up for Arnold. 'It is such a quaint, odd-proportioned place, with the ceilings all higgledy-piggledy and the view over the rooftops from the window: I know any boy would love it for his own.'

James, looking round at the higgledy-piggledy ceilings, thought that Aunt Fanny was perfectly right. In fact she sounded an absolutely splendid kind of aunt: the more he read the diary the more sure he felt that she would not have minded. It was almost, indeed, as though she was talking to him, in an enthusiastic, slightly breathless voice ... 'I am quite worn out, I do declare, with all my preparations. I have baked so much that we would withstand a *siege* I believe; let us hope the dear boy has a good appetite. Alas, the puppy has eaten my second-best bonnet but no matter—it is a dear thing, though I fear of somewhat mixed descent, the puppy I mean to say, not the bonnet which was of the best leghorn straw and a fine velvet trimming. But I would be indeed an unchristian soul were I to consider a living creature of less consequence than a mere hat.' He found himself feeling resentful towards Arnold and thinking that he'd jolly well better appreciate his luck in having such an excellent aunt, and not turn out to be some awful, wet, feeble kind of boy. He might well, with a name like that ...

But all was well. Arnold arrived, delivered from the mail-coach labelled all over like a parcel and with what Aunt Fanny called 'the most prodigious appetite in the world. I never knew a boy could eat so much at one sitting!' He was delighted with his room. 'He declared it was the most excellent place he ever saw, and was quite in *raptures*! Mr Timms the carpenter was only done the day before, and the plastering just complete, and the paint on the window still wet. It had been in a most dreadful condition, having been shut up many years, perhaps ever since this house was young, and that is quite an age ago. But now it is truly delightful: we have such charming paper on the walls, with a pattern of green leaves.'

Arnold settled down at once. He climbed the chestnut tree in the churchyard, and fell out of it. He named the puppy Palmerston after the Prime Minister and insisted that it slept on his bed. He ate everything Aunt Fanny provided, and proclaimed her the best cook in the world. He went with her to Oxford, and persuaded her into a boat on the river ... ('Declaring of course that he was quite used to handling a pair of oars, and then put us aground so that we stuck fast in the bank! I laughed till tears ran down my cheeks, and a fine sight we must have been, Arnold struggling to push the boat out and I in my good silk dress and my Sunday bonnet endeavouring my best to help ...'). They fished on the Evenlode: Aunt Fanny caught six perch and was ecstatic. They ate them for supper.

James warmed to Arnold. He seemed to have all the right ideas. James would, he thought regretfully, have got on with him. They'd have had a good time together, with that fishing-rod, and the puppy, and the sorties Arnold had made into the countryside which, in those days, wrapped itself much more closely around Ledsham. The cottage had been among fields, then. Looking round the room, thinking of Arnold seeing the same church tower framed in the window, the same tipping ceiling over the bed, he almost felt his noisy, cheerful presence. It came as a shock to realize that it was a hundred and twenty years since Arnold had stood in this room.

He turned back to the diary. Days passed: 'I cannot imagine how I occupied myself before Arnold came,' wrote Aunt Fanny. 'We are most agreeably busy. There is never a dull moment! Never a day goes by but the dear boy produces some new scheme for our entertainment. I had quite forgot what a variety of diversions the young have at their disposal. And I in my turn have done a little to instruct Arnold in the domestic arts for the dear boy being of an enquiring mind is not averse to learn how his favourite delicacies are made. He can make a passably good pie and also bake the plum and spice cakes of which he is so very fond.' And then suddenly a note of discord crept into the diary: a porcelain vase, much treasured by Aunt Fanny, had been mysteriously broken. Aunt Fanny did not say so in as many words, but it was clear from her wounded comments, that she suspected Arnold. And he made too much noise up in his room. 'I have had to remonstrate with him,' said Aunt Fanny severely, 'though he protested his innocence with the *greatest* force and conviction.' The puppy, too, was in disgrace. 'He has taken to barking at thin air: I wonder if the animal could perhaps be deranged?'

Things went from bad to worse. And then the messages began to come. James could imagine all too well how Arnold must have felt. 'My poor nephew told me that at first he suspected trickery by some other boy, but could think of none who might be responsible, and then *even* thought that I myself might have compounded some elaborate joke! The first note he found upon his pillow—a great missive all in antique script about how he should employ some queer magical method for the searching out of thieves, and how he should instruct me to infuse certain herbs for the treatment of my various ailments, and suchlike nonsense. The second he found written upon the copybook in which he keeps his daily journal, which threw the boy into quite a *rage* so that he brought the book at once to me and demanded who I thought could be plaguing him so. This message stated more clearly the writer's credentials, and was signed with his name—Thomas Kempe—with the *perplexing* information that he was—or thought himself to be—a *sorcerer*. I was as puzzled as Arnold, until I recalled that the humbler kind of person in these parts—the more uneducated, I mean to say—will still talk of a *sorcerer*, or a *wise man*, as one to whom a person might have recourse in time of trouble but this is an old sort of superstition and not much found today I believe even among the poor. But thinking of this and also upon all the *disturbances* that have troubled me of late and that I thought to be the doing of my poor nephew, it occurred to me all of a sudden that perhaps we were the object of some kind of *supernatural* manifestation and so in a great upset I put on my bonnet and *ran* straight to the Vicarage to consult with our good Vicar and ask his opinion ...'

Sensible Aunt Fanny. Lucky old Arnold, thought James, not to be stuck with grown-ups who just said, 'There's no such things as ghosts, and that's that.' Instead *he* had good old Aunt Fanny, who jumped at once to the right conclusion. For the Vicar immediately confirmed her suspicions. He examined the messages, visited the house (and was treated to an exhibition of Thomas Kempe's noisiest and most destructive habits), and proclaimed that this was indeed a case of infestation by poltergeist. The diary became even more incoherent than usual, so that it was rather difficult to unravel the events of the Vicar's visit from an outburst of exclamation marks and repetitions of things that had already happened or that Aunt Fanny had already talked about at great length, but at last he found himself reading the passage that had caught his eye when he first opened the diary. 'Truly I am so relieved that I threw myself upon the Vicar for advice for while he has not been able to solve our *problem* he has been able to tell us what it is we suffer from but something must be done quickly for the house has been set in quite an uproar by the creature ...'

Aunt Fanny and Arnold were soon busily involved in trying to get rid of their unwelcome visitor. 'We are resolved to say nothing of the matter to Arnold's mother. We are both agreed that while Mary is the most *admirable* soul in the world she is also very matter-of-fact in her thinking—even a trifle *set* in her opinions—and to put it frankly we think she would seek other explanations for what is undoubtedly a case of *haunting*. Arnold is certain of this: he says he often finds difficulty in convincing her that things are of one complexion when she is determined that they are of another.' (I know what he means, thought James with sympathy. Lucky she wasn't around, Arnold's mum. They'd have had two problems then.) 'However,' Aunt Fanny continued, 'the Vicar is *entirely* of our opinion and treats the affair as one of considerable gravity. He believes that the spirit was in some way released when I had the attic room opened up and prepared for Arnold's visit. How little I imagined such a thing when I chose the green-leafed wallpaper and bore home in triumph the little table to go by the bed! But now, all that matters is *what* is to be done to rid us of this wretched creature?'

The Vicar decided upon a solemn ritual with bell, book and candle, which, he assured them, was bound to do the trick. Aunt Fanny became incoherent again at the prospect. What were the social requirements of such an occasion? Should she serve cake and madeira? What should she wear? Her church-going clothes? Or would that perhaps be unsuitable? Should Arnold be allowed to be present, or not? (Arnold solved that problem himself. 'The boy absolutely insists, so vehemently that I really do not think I could keep him out.' I bet he did, thought James, you wouldn't want to miss a thing like that ...)

The exorcism took place on a Sunday afternoon. Those present were Aunt Fanny, Arnold, the Vicar's wife, in case Aunt Fanny should be overcome with nerves and require feminine support, and the Vicar, officiating. They all trooped up to the attic, drew the curtains, and embarked upon a lengthy ceremony, involving much incantation and exhortation by the Vicar, the details of which were lost in Aunt Fanny's confused

103

and excited recollections—'I scarce believed myself in my own house the Vicar was so very *sonorous* quite unlike his sermons of a Sunday which are delivered quite *simply* and there was good Mrs Ashe all of a twitch as indeed was I at what we might expect to see or hear ...'

What they saw was nothing. What they heard was a noisy expression of Thomas Kempe's displeasure, with doors banging, windows rattling, and all the candles being blown out. The Vicar was obliged to abandon his ritual speech. It was clearly having no effect at all. However, he was not a man to admit defeat, it appeared. He declared that he had an alternative method in reserve, and demanded a bottle with a stout cork ... Arnold volunteered to find one from my store cupboard. 'The boy was impressed I'm sure by the solemnity of the occasion but his eyes sparkled so and he watched so close that I must confess I think he found it a rare treat also ...'

And this time they were successful. 'The Vicar exhorted the spirit again though I fear I was so stirred up his words passed quite over my head and then there was a silence and we scarce dared take a breath and then all of a sudden we saw a little blue flame pass over the table, quite like the flicker of marsh-gas or even a glow-worm—quite as pale as that, and lo! it went *into* the bottle and vanished and there was a great *stillness* as though something was at peace and the Vicar corked up the bottle and declared that all was done ...'

And that, so far as Aunt Fanny and Arnold were concerned, was that. They never heard Thomas Kempe again, and there were no more messages. 'Arnold,' wrote Aunt Fanny, 'was most indignant that I should wish to shut up the attic room once more. He declared that he would cry fiddle! and snap his fingers at the creature now it was thus laid and disposed of, but I insisted, and in this instance I had my way. The room is shut up once more, pretty wallpaper and all, and the bottle is put in a crevice in the wall below the window, and the place plastered over, for this is what the Vicar said we must do, and there so far as I am concerned it will stay for ever.'

9

James put the diary down and looked around him, feeling slightly dazed. It was something of a shock to see his room quite normal and ordinary, football boots hanging from the hook behind the door, pyjamas protruding from under the pillow, books, pictures, all in the proper place. No green and white wallpaper, no Aunt Fanny chattering on breathlessly, no Arnold watching with sparkling eyes as the Rector intoned his stern words for the dismissal of Thomas Kempe. Nothing there. Just an old diary, yellow, tattered, blotched with damp. James, who was not given to sentiment, sat and stared out of the window, and a very odd lumpy feeling, like the beginning of a cold, came into the back of his throat.

'James! Supper!'

Could it really be? He must have been reading for ages and ages. He put the diary away very carefully in the drawer of his table, under a pile of exercise books and his Study on Beetles, and went downstairs. Arnold, too, had clattered down these same stairs, in response to Aunt Fanny's summonses. Arnold had sat in the same kitchen, eating Aunt Fanny's gargantuan meals. Aunt Fanny had had misgivings about this: she had thought it more suitable to eat in the parlour but had capitulated to Arnold, who preferred the kitchen, and there, cosily, they had eaten, facing each other across the scrubbed deal table. Here, too, Arnold had been made, protesting, to bath in the tin hip bath—an elaborate business involving much heating of coppers on the stove and warming of towels before the fire and general bustling about. Had Arnold known about the way on to the roof? Had he and Palmerston hunted for rats in the old drain by the fence? Had he preferred the sharp, sweet apples or the big, soft, floury ones?

But that, and many more things, James would never know, and thinking about it gave him an odd, lonely, deprived feeling so that he ate his meal in silence, hardly listening to the conversation that went on round him. Just once he lifted his head from the beefburgers and chips to say, 'What's Cumberland Pudding, Mum?'

'I'm not too sure. I think it was a Victorian dish.'

'Could we have it some time?'

It had been one of Arnold's favourites.

The next day Arnold and Aunt Fanny were still very much in his thoughts but his feelings about them had matured so that to think of them was less sorrowful and more warmly companiable. To know about them, to know what they had said and done and thought, was to have a friendship with them which, curiously enough, did not feel entirely onesided, though the only real link between them was the unwelcome one of Thomas Kempe. Ploughing through the long grass in the orchard, James could close his eyes and imagine Arnold at his side (in knickerbockers which rubbed his legs—he had complained loudly and often to Aunt Fanny about them—and black boots which he hated and had once lost in the mud of the river bank). James told Arnold a joke about two flies on a ceiling that he had heard at school and Arnold, a hundred years away, laughed and shouted and swung on the branch of an apple tree.

'Why on earth are you talking to yourself?' said Simon.

James looked up, startled. Simon must have come right up

without him hearing. He stood, staring at James through his round spectacles. James separated himself from Arnold—reluctantly, but Arnold would be there again when he needed him—and came back to here and now.

'Was I?'

'Yes.'

'Oh,' said James. 'Oh well, never mind.' He thought of telling Simon about Arnold and Aunt Fanny, showing him the diary, sharing it all, and almost in the same moment rejected the idea. It was no reflection on Simon to know, quite simply, that he could never understand the total involvement James felt with Arnold and Aunt Fanny: it was something private, inexplicable, and very personal. It seemed even more impossible to expect other people to understand a very real rush of feeling about a boy you had never met and never would meet, than to ask them to believe in an active poltergeist. But, happily, there was no need to explain Arnold.

Simon said, 'I'm going fishing. Want to come?'

James hesitated, tempted. Fishing in the Evenlode would be forever associated, now, with Arnold, but it would be no betrayal of him to go and do it with Simon. Arnold was one kind of friend: Simon another. There was plenty of room for both of them.

'Well, yes,' he began. 'Hang on while I get my boots.' And then he remembered. Bert Ellison. He was coming again today —would be here any minute. Crumbs, James thought, how could I have forgotten?

'No,' he said. 'I must be going barmy. The exorcist is coming again.' With a burst of generosity he added, 'You can stay and watch this time, if you like.'

But Simon's thoughts were concentrated on fishing. He said he didn't think he would, thanks all the same, and departed, leaving James with the feeling, once more, that he did not really take the sorcerer seriously enough. But there was Arnold now, and Arnold had taken it seriously all right. He'd jolly well had to, hadn't he?

Bert Ellison was propping his bike against the fence as James came round the front of the house. He had a small, forked branch under one arm and was whistling the theme tune from a popular film.

'How's he been keeping, then, your chap?' he said. 'Cooking up anything new?'

'Not really,' said James. He lowered his voice and said, 'I think I know why it didn't work last time, though.'

'Do you now?' said Bert. 'Well, let's be getting up there and you can tell me all about it, eh?'

They went upstairs.

'Where's your mum?'

'Out. She won't be back till supper.'

'Just as well,' said Bert. 'We don't want to be disturbed. And she's a lady that knows what's what, your mum. Or reckons she does. No offence meant, mind.'

As soon as they were in the room, with the door firmly closed (Helen was around somewhere) James got out the diary, and began to explain. He read aloud the last entry, about the final exorcism (Bert had left his glasses behind) and Bert listened carefully, his expression registering interest but no surprise.

'I reckoned we might have got one of those on our hands,' he said finally. 'One of them persistent beggars. And they learn from experience, there's no getting away from it. No, we'd never have got him again with the bottle. Wasting our time, we was.' He was rolling up the rug from the centre of the floor, and pushing back the table.

'What are you doing?' said James nervously.

'We've got to clear space for the circle, haven't we? What would your mother say to the odd chalk mark on the floor, do you think?'

'I don't think she'd be very pleased.'

'Well, we'd better not go causing trouble, I suppose. We'll have to make do with paper and pencil, though it should be chalk, properly speaking.' He delved in his overall pocket, and brought out a pencil, and then an envelope and contents which he was about to tear into pieces when he looked more closely and said, 'No. That's my football coupon, I'll be wanting that.'

'I've got some paper,' said James.

'Let's have it then.'

Bert tore a sheet of paper into eight pieces, sat down at the table, and pencilled on each one a series of indecipherable marks and scrawls, breathing heavily as he did so.

'What do they mean?' said James.

'Ah,' said Bert, 'now you're asking me. I had them from my dad, to tell the truth. He did a bit in this line, from time to time. I couldn't exactly tell you what they mean, but they've been known to work, and that's a fact.'

He placed the eight pieces of paper in a circle in the centre of the floor, weighting each one down with a nail from his toolbox. In the middle of the circle he put the forked rowan stick, propped against a chair. Then he walked over to the curtains, peered up at the top of them, and said, 'Drat it, these has got some sort of modern nonsense. It's the old-fashioned kind we need.'

'What?' said James, bewildered.

'A curtain ring, son. We need a brass curtain ring. Can you fix us up with one of them?'

'I 'spect so,' said James. He bolted down the stairs, dashed into the sitting-room, rummaged in his mother's work-drawer, found what he was looking for and was gone up the stairs again while Helen was still saying plaintively, 'Shut the door, can't you, there's a beastly draught again.'

Bert placed the curtain ring over the pointed end of the

stick, so that it slipped down the fork. Then he stepped away from the circle, motioned James back with his hand, cleared his throat loudly and said, 'Thomas Kempe! Are you there?'

James, who had not expected such a direct approach, was startled. This seemed a far remove from the elaborate proceedings of Aunt Fanny and Arnold, or, indeed, from Bert's own first attempt to engage the sorcerer's attention.

Nothing happened. Bert coughed, adjusted one of the pieces of paper and said, 'Enter the circle, and let us speak with you. Come!'

'What happens if he does?' whispered James.

'It'll do for him. The rowan, see. Rowan's no good for chaps like him. But you got to get him in there first.' Downstairs, a door banged, and somewhere outside Tim was barking.

'Thomas Kempe! I summon you!' said Bert severely. One of the pieces of paper lifted at the edge, as though examined by a curious breeze. There was a creak, that might or might not have been the shifting of ancient timbers. Bert said, in a murmur, 'He's biting! No doubt about it. This is where we got to go carefully. You've got to play them like a fish at this stage, see.'

James, stiff with excitement, told Arnold to come quick and watch, and Arnold came from the Evenlode, or up the apple tree, or rabbiting in the field with Palmerston or wherever he had been and stood by James and shared feelings and thoughts and the large, comfortable presence of Bert Ellison and the draughty, uncertain one of Thomas Kempe.

Down below, the front gate clicked and someone came up the path.

'Your mum?' said Bert.

'No,' said James. Footsteps are like voices, instantly known. 'It'll be someone collecting or something. Helen'll go.' He was staring at the rowan stick: was it moving, quivering just a little?

'You have a word with him,' said Bert. 'After all, it's you seem to have set him off in the first place.'

The last time I did that, thought James, it didn't turn out very well. Maybe the nature of this occasion would put their relationship somehow on a safer basis. With his eyes riveted on the stick (surely the ring twitched just then?) he said diffidently, 'Are you there?'

The stick shook. One of the nails rolled off its piece of paper.

'Ah,' said Bert. 'Go on.'

'Please could I talk to you?' said James more confidently. A small fist of air wandered across the back of his neck and the stick shook again, nudging the back of the chair. Downstairs, the front door opened and closed. There were voices in the hall—Helen and somebody else, but he hadn't time to listen.

'You're doing fine,' said Bert. 'Carry on like this and I'll be out of a job.'

'I wanted to ask you ...' said James intensely, and the stick rubbed up and down again and the ring caught a strip of sunlight and flashed at him. The voices were louder.

'I wanted to ask if ...' and then suddenly the voices were on the landing below and coming up the stairs and it was Helen and Mrs Verity and Mrs Verity was saying '... so if you don't mind dear I'll just pop up and have a word with him while he's here.'

The stick fell over with a clatter. The curtains bellied out into the room as the window burst open under a roll of air pressure. Mrs Verity and Helen came in as Bert was kicking the stick hastily under the bed and sweeping up the pieces of paper in one hand.

'I didn't want to be a nuisance but I knew Mrs Harrison wouldn't mind me taking the liberty,' said Mrs Verity, 'since I saw your bike outside, Bert. I just wanted to say if you've a moment to spare later in the week I've got a window broken round the back. Could you fix it for me, do you think? I'd be ever so grateful.'

'We'll see what we can do,' said Bert. He took a steel measure out of his pocket and ran it along the wall, with a thoughtful look on his face. James stood stock still where he was, trying to suppress the gusts of feeling that threatened to make him do something he might regret later. Mrs Verity was looking round the room with interest.

'This is a nice little place you've got up here, dear.'

'Yes,' muttered James to the floor.

Mrs Verity looked injured. 'Well, I hope I'm not intruding. I don't want to be in the way I'm sure.'

'Dear me, no. We're glad of a bit of company, aren't we?' said Bert cheerfully and James took a deep breath and said, 'Yes, that's right.'

Mrs Verity brightened. She sat down on James' chair and talked for five minutes while Bert got on with putting up the shelves and said 'Oh, ay,' and 'Fancy that, now' in the right places and James stared dolefully at the window. Once, she said, 'Come to think of it, dear, weren't we talking about Bert the other day, you and me?'

'Were we?' said James. 'I can't remember, actually.'

'Maybe it was somebody else. You get a bit absentminded as you get older, that's one thing I do find. Well, I must be getting on. You won't forget, will you, Bert?'

'Count on me,' said Bert.

When she had gone James said in anguish, 'We'd nearly got him, hadn't we?'

'Could be. And again could be not. There's no telling.'

'Can we try again?'

'What, the same bag 'o tricks? No, there wouldn't be no point in that. I've told you, they learn by experience, these chaps.'

'Bother Mrs Verity. Oh, *bother* her. He can't stand her, you see. He says she's a witch.'

'That's going a bit far,' said Bert.

'I know.'

Bert got on with the shelves and James handed him nails and tried not to think about anything at all. There is absolutely no point in blaming somebody for something they don't even know they've done, and anyway, as Bert said, it might not have worked. All the same, he couldn't help feeling very gloomy and frustrated.

At last Bert finished the shelves and they went downstairs. Outside the front gate he said, 'Well, I'm sorry all that come to nothing again. We'll forget about the charge, being as how I wasn't able to deal with him. Anyhow, you got your shelves.'

'Yes,' said James. Then he added, 'Thank you very much for trying.'

'Don't look so put out. Maybe we'll come up with something yet. I'll keep on having a think about it, and you let me know if you got any news. The more you know about the chap you're dealing with, the better. I've got a job on in the church for the next couple of weeks, so you'll know where to find me if you want me.'

'Yes. Thanks. I will.'

'Cheerio, then.'

' 'Bye,' said James.

A wretched evening followed. Part of the trouble could be put down to Thomas Kempe, who roamed the house till bedtime, slamming doors, knocking over the hall table, and disrupting the television, which made Mr and Mrs Harrison tetchy. The rest of it was attributable to James himself, who felt too disgruntled to be tactful and eventually got himself sent up early with the threat of no outing at half-term. Upstairs, he shared his troubles with Arnold and Arnold agreed how jolly unfair it all was (he knew all about problems of that kind: Aunt Fanny of course was the most splendid and understanding person in the world and hardly ever got in a bad temper about anything but Arnold's father had been another matter altogether) and messages went to and fro between them until at last James fell asleep and dreamed of a long hot summer day full of rivers and willow trees and picnic baskets stuffed with delicacies and, of course, the company of Arnold, with Aunt Fanny benignly in the background.

10

The next day, something dreadful happened. Something that, while less positively destructive or untidy than the sorcerer's previous activities, outdid them all in sheer malignity.

It was Helen who saw it first. She had set off for school a few minutes before James, and came running back almost at once. She burst into the kitchen, looking a size larger than usual in the way of people who have a piece of shattering and as yet unshared information.

'Come and see what someone's done to Mrs Verity's fence!'

The Harrisons trooped outside. James gazed in horror. Thomas Kempe had, clearly, taken a tip from the football enthusiasts and other graffiti writers who occasionally plastered Ledsham walls with their comments and invocations. Along the length of Mrs Verity's garden fence was chalked, in white letters a foot high

WIDDOW VERITIE IS A WYTCHE

One or two other early passers-by had paused for a moment to stare curiously. And, of course, Mrs Verity herself had come out to see what the fuss was about. She arrived outside her gate at the same moment as the Harrisons hurried across the road. They had hoped to prevent her seeing it. The expression on her face filled James with a burst of impotent fury at the sorcerer.

'That's not nice,' said Mrs Verity, her voice wavering. 'That's not at all nice, that isn't.'

'There,' said Mrs Harrison, 'come over to us and have a cup of tea. The children will get a bucket of water and have it all cleaned up before you go back.'

James and Helen sloshed and scrubbed. The writing came off pretty easily. How fortunate, James thought, that Thomas Kempe hadn't discovered about aerosol paints. That'll be the day, he said to himself gloomily. And in the awful and inexorable march of events it seemed bound to come.

'What a mean thing to do,' said Helen. 'Who do you reckon it was? Have another go at the "wytch" bit—you can still see it just.'

'Dunno,' said James, scrubbing. 'Vandals,' he added, after a moment.

Helen said wisely. 'I s'pose so. They couldn't spell, whoever they were.'

By the time they got back to their own house, Mrs Verity was slowly recovering, fortified by tea and sympathy.

'It gives you a nasty feeling,' she was saying plaintively. 'Having people think badly of you behind your back.'

Mrs Harrison made soothing noises, poured more tea.

'Doing a thing like that. It makes you feel all queer.'

'Hooligans,' said Mr Harrison.

'I've always got on well enough with people.'

'Young thugs. Contemptible. One ignores them.'

'Tried to be neighbourly.' A large white handkerchief came out of Mrs Verity's apron pocket as her voice quavered again.

'Of course you have,' said Mrs Harrison. 'And it was just some stupid louts and nobody's taken any notice.'

'You can't see it at all now,' said Helen.

'Thank you my dear. I'm very grateful, I'm sure.' The white handkerchief was lowered. James would have liked to contribute comfort of some kind, but he only had a gob-stopper in his pocket, coated with fluff, which seemed an inadequate offering.

'I'd better be getting back,' said Mrs Verity. 'There's all the dishes in the sink still.'

'I'll come over later and see you're all right,' said Mrs Harrison.

'That's very kind. It's made me nervous, that, it really has. I'll have a lie down, I think.'

When Mrs Verity had gone Mr Harrison delivered a short lecture about thuggery and hooliganism and the dangers of idle and undirected youth which the children rather resented as it seemed in some way aimed towards them and indeed was, since it turned out that his purpose was to utter a stern warning that any such inclinations on their part would be firmly and summarily dealt with. He was only halted by Helen pointing out, in silken tones, that they were already a quarter of an hour late for school.

'It's not fair,' she said, as they turned out of the gate. 'We're not like that. Even you aren't. You only break windows by accident.'

'Thanks,' said James.

'At least I s'pose you do. They must have done it in the night, that writing. It's funny you didn't hear anything—it's right opposite your window.'

'Vandals are like burglars,' said James. 'Dead quiet.'

There was little time to think again about things during the day. The school was about to celebrate its centenary and Mr Hollings had decided to put on a grand exhibition of its history. It was called 'A Hundred Years of State Education' and had involved much coming and going amongst the older inhabitants of Ledsham to dig out anything that was relevant to the early days of the school. The hall was full of old text books, vast black leather-bound Registers and Log Books, tattered exercise books, and yellowing photographs of smock-clad, black-booted boys and girls staring bun-faced at the camera under the stern gaze of ladies in ankle-length dresses and straw boaters. All this had to be arranged on trestle-tables, along with displays of the kind of work done nowadays, and in the fuss and bustle James was completely taken up with problems of lettering notices and covering tables with sheets of white paper. The school was to be opened for the day in two days' time, so that Ledsham might see the exhibition.

Mr Hollings spent half the afternoon perched on the edge of a table, absorbed in the Log Book for 1873. Occasionally he read bits aloud to anyone who was within earshot.

'Listen to this. "September 12th. No children have come to school this past two weeks on account of the harvest."'

Someone said, 'Lucky things.'

'Not at all,' said Mr Hollings tersely. 'They were going to spend the rest of their lives harvesting, most of them. "January 12th. Ellen Gibson was late again and was beaten. The snow is two feet deep in the back lanes and the children are all day with wet feet. Miss Fanny Spence brought a bag of coal for the stove."'

'What?' said James, dropping the scissors.

'Mmn?' said Mr Hollings, turning over the page.

'Please,' said James breathlessly, 'could you read that bit again. About Miss Fanny Spence.'

Mr Hollings did so.

'Is that all?'

'Yes. She's cropped up once before, if I remember. Yes, here she is in June, bringing a basket of cakes to be distributed among the children. She seems to have been a kindly soul.'

They might have been her special plum and spice cakes, James thought, the ones Arnold had been so very partial to. Maybe Arnold had put her up to it, knowing what the children would like. And then, thinking about dates, he realised with a start that this was nearly twenty years later than the diary.

Aunt Fanny must have been an old lady, and Arnold—Arnold was grown-up.

'Relation of yours?' said Mr Hollings.

'No. No, not really.'

Mrs Verity was more or less herself again by the time James got home in the afternoon. The Harrisons had all promised to keep a vigilant eye on the street, especially at night. Tim would be posted outside the gate as a watch-dog.

'What a commotion,' said Mrs Harrison. 'Where are you going, James?'

'Fishing with Simon.'

'Don't be late for supper.'

James was worried. He told Simon about Mrs Verity's fence.

Simon said, 'That was a mean thing to do.'

'I know. That's why I'm dead worried. He's not just getting at me now.'

Simon said kindly, 'Anyway, they won't think it's you. *I* don't think it's you.'

'Meaning you have other times?'

'Well—' Simon sounded uncomfortable, as well he might —'At the beginning I did sort of wonder ... I mean, it could have been a joke.'

'A hilarious one. Specially funny for me.'

'It's because of not really believing in ghosts. Or at least only half. Who do they think it was, then?'

'Vandals. People who bash up 'phone boxes and that.'

'Well,' said Simon brightly, 'p'raps it was.'

James felt all of a sudden very weary. He said, 'All right, then, p'raps it was. Have it your own way.' He was on his own, where Thomas Kempe was concerned, and that was a fact. And it was getting worse, now that he was turning his attentions to other people, such as harmless old Mrs Verity. If only she could know, James thought, what she did—coming up to my room yesterday. If she hadn't turned up just then we might have got rid of him, Bert and me. But now? Now Thomas Kempe seemed strengthened. Strengthened and becoming dangerously independent.

With all this on his mind the pleasure of fishing was rather blunted, he found. Moreover the fishing rod was Simon's, and with the best will in the world two people cannot satisfactorily share a fishing-rod. So after half an hour or so he left Simon and wandered off into the fields with Tim.

It was a golden afternoon. The hedgerows lay in neat black lines among bleached fields of stubble and sunshine came through them in spurts. Long black fingers of shade streamed away from the elms on the hilltop and the whole wide arc of the horizon was fringed with the blue and graceful shapes of trees against the pale sky. James walked along an overgrown lane, between margins rusty with docks and the fine tracery of dried cow-parsley heads, and before long Arnold came to join him and together they went into the copse by the farm and ate blackberries while Tim and Palmerston rooted in the undergrowth and pigeons lumbered overhead. Arnold knew a place where there'd once been a quarry: it was all green and bushy now, but you could slide down the steep sides and swing Tarzan-like among branches from one side to the other (Arnold didn't know about Tarzan: James had to explain but he got the idea at once). They did this until the sky flamed orange behind the trees and then drained to pale lemon and finally turquoise and there was a thin flat light in the wood and rooks homing across the fields. Then James said he'd better be getting back or there'd be a fuss and they walked down the lane together and somewhere on the edge of the village Arnold went away and James came on home by himself.

Home was warm and stuffy and smelt of liver and bacon for supper. James came in quietly because there were things wrong with his jeans and sweater and a lot of dirt around which he had to do something about before his mother saw him.

He went upstairs with his head still full of space and sky and the shifting patterns of leaves, and his hands numb from the hard-soft touch of tree-trunks: he passed Helen half-way up and she stared at him and said 'Why on earth were you shouting "Palmerston!" at Tim just then?' and he looked at her without really hearing and went on to the bathroom.

He turned the tap on and as he did so the door closed on him with a decisive slam. With a sinking feeling he recognized the symptoms of Thomas Kempe's presence—the restless expectancy that possessed a room, the sense of intrusion, the insistent pressure of a self-important, opinionated personality. James thought that there were still plenty of people like that around (he could think of one or two): but maybe the way things were arranged now they didn't get the chance to do so much meddling. Or did they? Maybe they did, in different ways and places. Wearily, he turned the tap off and waited.

The message was on the floor, written on a wedge of paper that had been used to stop the window rattling. James unrolled it and read:

Goe & tell they that are diggynge for treasure in the Lammas Fields that they must give me one halfe of what they finde for it is I who tell where gold may be found in these partes. Doe this at once or it will be the worse for thee.

At first he was puzzled as well as angry. Then the sorcerer's meaning dawned on him. He hesitated, considered banging out of the room and going downstairs, decided that might be asking for trouble, and settled for a direct answer.

He said out loud, 'Look, they aren't looking for treasure. People don't nowadays—they've got football pools and things instead. They're archaeologists. And it's not gold they're digging up—it's a lot of broken pots.' Anyway, he added under his breath, even if it was you wouldn't have much use for it now, would you?

The room paused: it seemed to digest the information and then spit it straight back at him. A bottle of shampoo fell off the shelf and broke. The medicine cabinet on the wall shook dangerously.

'Oh, all right,' shouted James. 'All right, I'll go. But not now. I can't go out again tonight—they'd never let me. See?'

There was a stillness, a hovering, and then Thomas Kempe apparently accepted the compromise for all of a sudden the room emptied and became quite ordinary and uncomplicated, leaving James alone with the smell of toothpaste and a mess of glass and shampoo on the floor that would have to be explained. He finished washing and went downstairs, feeling persecuted.

All day at school he wondered uneasily if the sorcerer was capable of appreciating the fact that he wouldn't be able to carry out his wishes until the afternoon. And he hadn't the slightest idea what he was going to say or do when he got there, either. He'd have to face that problem when it arose.

He asked Simon to come with him. Arnold would have been glad to, he felt sure, but—well, he preferred to keep Arnold for private and more unworried times. And there was always the possibility that Simon might be some practical help.

'You can't just tell them to stop it. Why should they take any notice?'

'I know.'

'What are you going to do then?'

'I'm hoping I'll think of something before we get there,' said James crossly.

The archæologists' field was half a mile or so from the village. By the time the boys reached the edge of it James could feel Thomas Kempe's nagging presence: there was nothing to be seen or heard, but a claustrophobic atmosphere of perversity and obsession descended upon them so that

124

although the autumn day was as golden as the one before it was as though they were no longer able to see it: there was nothing remarkable about the splayed shapes of the elms along the skyline, or the glowing chestnut leaves under their feet. They quarrelled about which direction they should take.

The archaeologists were unwelcoming. Two of them were sitting at the edge of the field making complicated notes. They waved the boys away. The third, young and bearded, was sitting at the edge of a shallow hole doing things with a steel measure. He was a student, it appeared, and a little more forthcoming. James decided to hold him in conversation: perhaps the sorcerer could be fooled somehow.

There were broken pots in the hole. And bones.

'What are they?' said James.

'It's a burial ground. That was a pot they put in graves.'

'What are you going to do with it?'

'It'll be put together again, and fetch up in a museum.'

'And the bones?'

'Couldn't say really.'

At the bottom of the field the river made a small rushing noise at a twist in the bank. These people might have heard that noise, too, when they'd been around. James said, faintly disapproving, 'Do you think it's all right, digging people up like that?'

'What?'

'I think you ought to leave them alone.'

'It's got to be recorded,' said the student. 'Far as I'm concerned, it's a Middle Bronze Age primary cremation burial, with bucket-urn and cremated bones.'

'As far as I'm concerned, it's people,' said James. The student began to sort out the bits of pot and bone. He put the bones into a plastic bag, and the whole lot into a cardboard carton stamped Lux Toilet Soap 12 x 20, Open This End.

There was a disturbance just behind them. A small folding

table, with more boxes, and papers and drawing-boards, toppled over.

'Here,' said the student angrily. 'Mind what you're doing.'

'We didn't,' said Simon.

'Well, you could have fooled me. Blast. I'd just sorted all those sherds.'

They began to pick things up. The papers swirled in a sudden breeze.

'Look out,' said the student. 'They're going to be in the river if we don't watch it.'

James grabbed flying sheets of paper. Over the top of them, he said to the sky, 'Stop digging in the Lammas fields. Give half the gold you find to Thomas Kempe.'

'What's that?' said the student.

'Nothing.'

'Put that stuff back on the table, would you. Hope this wind doesn't mean the weather's going to break—we're supposed to be here another couple of weeks.'

'I expect it does,' said James.

'Cheerful, aren't you?'

'Do you like digging people up?'

'It's not a question of like or not like,' said the student shortly. 'I've got my Finals next summer.'

'I was only asking.'

'Sorry. I've got a cracking headache all of a sudden. Oughtn't you two to be getting along home?'

'Look out,' said Simon. The student, stepping sideways beside his hole, tripped against a stone that didn't seem to have been there before, staggered, and fetched up with one foot in the hole. There was a crumbling sound as pieces of pottery disintegrated further.

'Oh, God,' said the student. The two men at the far side of the field had looked up. Now they were coming across.

James said to Simon that he thought they'd better go, and

Simon said maybe they had. As they climbed over the gate into the road they could hear the two men saying things to the student in loud, aggressive voices. There were still pieces of paper flapping about on the grass.

'I expect that's mucked up his finals,' said Simon. 'But it wasn't our fault.'

James nodded. He was thinking, secretly, that maybe it was a just reward for someone who sorted bits of other people out into cardboard boxes: anyway, he didn't care all that much. And Thomas Kempe had gone—he could feel that. The sky was higher and wider and bluer and the sprays of red berries in the hedgerows were suddenly one of the best things he'd ever seen. He thought of telling Arnold to come, and then decided to save him up for later.

'He won't be pleased,' said Simon. 'Your old Thomas Whatsit.'

'Bother him.'

They went back slowly, because there were various things to be done on the way, among the willows on the river bank and in the big field where the stone wall was low enough to jump over if you took a good enough run at it. And then the fields ended and became the tidy fences and matching rooftops of the new housing estate and the bridle-path developed a tarmac surface and they were in Ledsham again. They came out of the housing estate and into the High Street, hurrying because the church clock had just struck and it was later than they'd thought. There was a police car parked outside the chemist's and a few people standing around staring at something. Simon wanted to go and investigate but James was thinking hard about tea and the fact that if he didn't get back soon Helen would have had all the cake, if there was any, and dragged him past. They went round the corner into Pound Lane and on the double doors of the Fire Station was chalked, in letters a foot high

'Oh, no!' said James.

Simon stared. He looked at James and then back at the Fire Station. He said, 'P'raps you'd better rub it off?'

'Are you daft? Someone might come, and it'll look as though I did it.'

As they went round the corner the police car came behind them. It slowed up as it went past the Fire Station, and then passed them and turned into the Oxford road. There were two policemen in it, and they both looked hard at the boys.

'See?' said James.

He had been at the Vicarage, too. On the front door was written THE PRIEST IS A LIAR & A SCOUNDREL. Again, he'd signed his name.

Simon was beginning to look thoroughly alarmed. Alarmed and bewildered. James crossed over to the other side of the road and hurried past, only glancing at it casually, as though it didn't interest him much.

They turned into East End Lane. In the distance there was a police car parked. Outside the Harrisons' house.

The policeman was in the sitting-room. Helen was sitting on the sofa, looking upset. Mr and Mrs Harrison were standing in front of the fireplace, reading a piece of paper that Mr Harrison was holding.

'James.'

'Yes, Dad.'

'I think you'd better have a look at this.'

James breathed deeply and said, 'What is it?'

'It's something that came through the window of the chemist's shop. Wrapped round a brick.'

James took the sheet of paper, which was a sheet from his personal notebook, and read, 'Doe not meddle in my businesse or I will worke your ende. James Harrison at East End Cott. will tell you why.'

Everybody watched him. Nobody spoke. Then Mr Harrison said, 'Well?'

Outside the window James could see Tim lurking by the front gate, eyeing the police car. Mrs Verity was sitting in her doorway. The starlings were lined up on the roof, observing.

'I think,' said James slowly, 'there must be somebody around who wants to get me into trouble.'

'And who might that be, do you imagine?'

The starlings pointed their beaks up at the blue sky and whistled. Mrs Verity knitted. James looked at the policeman, and the policeman looked back with a blank, neutral face.

'I don't know, really,' said James. There was a silence. And then inspiration came to him. 'What time did the chemist's window get broken?' The policeman's face looked suddenly more personal, reminding him that policemen are used to doing the asking, so he added, 'Please.'

'It was about five,' said the policeman.

'Then I was down by the river,' said James. 'Me and Simon. I mean Simon and I. We went to see those archaeologist people straight after school.'

'Talk to them?'

'Yes, one of them.'

'And when did you come back?'

'I'm not sure. Just now, really.'

'See anyone you know?'

'No. I mean, yes. Mr Hollings was just driving into his garage when we went through the estate and he waved to us.'

Relief filled the room. Mrs Harrison stopped standing to attention by the fireplace and sat down with a bump. Mr Harrison lit his pipe. Helen said, 'Typical!'

'I should think that lets you out, then,' said the policeman.

'Oh,' said James. 'Good.'

'Anybody you've had a quarrel with lately? Any of the lads?'

'Not really,' said James.

'Sure?'

'Quite sure.'

The policeman turned to Mr Harrison. 'Sorry about this, sir. I'll have to check of course, but if he's telling the truth I don't think he can have had anything to do with it.'

'I quite understand,' said Mr Harrison. 'Don't mention it.'

'Cup of tea?' said Mrs Harrison.

'No thank you madam. I'll have to get on.'

The policeman went. Tim came in. Mrs Verity moved her chair to watch the policeman drive down the street.

'*I'd* like some tea,' said James. 'If I'm being asked.'

'You must have had a fight with someone,' said Helen. 'Someone who's getting at you. Bigger boys.' It was the third time she'd said it.

'No,' said James. 'Not that I know of.' He sounded resigned. In fact, he was worried. He'd been lucky, that time. But what next?

'Aren't you angry?'

'No. I mean yes. Jolly angry. I'll have to find out who it was and sort them out.'

Helen gave him a long, suspicious look. 'You aren't. You're not angry at all. You don't sound like you, in fact.'

James said, 'P'raps I'm sickening for something. The plague, I should think. I shouldn't get too near me.' He went out into the orchard and stalked around the apple trees in the dusk, his head packed with huge, gloomy thoughts. The immediate future seemed appallingly dangerous: the house was square and black behind him against a violet sky and inside it there lurked the presence of Thomas Kempe like some kind of malevolent spider, hatching destruction. And Arnold, who he needed—Arnold had retreated into the immeasurable distances he came from and was climbing trees or fishing or eating Cumberland pudding in the sunlit June of 1856.

Leaving me stuck here on my own, thought James. Or just about on my own. There's only Simon and Bert Ellison. And Simon doesn't believe it: in fact I think he thinks it's me. And Bert believes but he can't help. He sighed, and went into the house, leaving the garden to the bats flittering above the trees and Tim, skulking away down the fence into the fields on some private nocturnal engagement.

In school next day Mr Hollings made a solemn announcement. There was a person, he said, or persons, going around Ledsham writing things on walls. Unpleasant, threatening

131

things about real people. Such as the Vicar, and the doctor, and the district nurse. And over and beyond that, windows had been broken at the chemist's and stones had been thrown at the car of the archaeologists working at City Farm. The children listened, and looked appropriately shocked. Mr Hollings continued that while he of course thought it quite preposterous that any of *his* children should be mixed up in anything so disgraceful, nevertheless he'd promised the police that he would mention the matter. Did anybody know anything about it?

A hundred heads shook.

Mr Hollings said that he hadn't expected that they would. But he knew they would agree that this had got to stop, and so he was going to ask everyone to keep an eye out and let him, or the police, know at once if they had any ideas about who was doing it. Would they do that?

A hundred heads nodded.

And now, said Mr Hollings, they must get on. There was a lot to be done today, finishing off the arrangements for the centenary celebrations.

On the way back to the classroom James found Mr Hollings beside him.

'James?'

'Yes.'

'The policeman had a word with me this morning.'

'Oh,' said James. A warm tide crept slowly up his neck and over his face.

'I said I saw you and Simon last night. Must have been just the time someone put that brick through the chemist's window.'

'Oh,' said James. 'Thank you.'

'So that lets you off.'

'Yes. I s'pose it does.'

'Funny thing,' said Mr Hollings. 'This writing, on walls

and that. There's something odd about it. Kind of old-fashioned. Bit like that stuff you put up on the board the other day. That little joke of yours.'

'Is it?' said James.

'Yes. You *don't* know anything about it, do you?'

'No.'

'I'm not suggesting anything, mind. I just wondered. Thought maybe you might know someone. Some person who might have done it.'

'No,' said James sadly. 'Not anyone. Not a person.'

'Ah. I see. Oh well ...'

Mr Hollings went away to sort out a disturbance at the other side of the classroom, leaving James with a feeling that he was not exactly under suspicion, but somehow faintly clouded. There was doubt around: nothing you could put your finger on, just the flavour of doubt. And that's not very nice, thought James, in fact it's not at all nice.

However, Mr Hollings came back later on, as though to repair their relationship. 'Just do a job for me, will you, James? We'd better have the benefactor's portrait up, I suppose. Could you get it out for me. You and Simon. It's that great big thing at the back of the stockroom.'

'Yes,' said James. 'Of course. What is the benefactor?'

'Oh, he's someone who gave things to the school. Ages ago. Money and books and that. Careful of the glass, won't you?'

'Yes,' said James.

The picture was under shelves of exercise books and cleaning things, with its face to the wall. They had to manoeuvre it past several boxes of nativity play costumes before they could get it out. It was heavy.

'Better dust it,' said Simon. 'Here, catch.'

James scrubbed at the glass with a duster. The bewhiskered face of an elderly man looked out at him: waterfalls of hair threatened to engulf his features, moustache, sideburns, beard, flowing down to a high cravat, stopping short of the watch-chain stretched across a substantial stomach.

'Who is he?' said Simon.

James peered at the gold plaque under the picture.

'What's the matter?' said Simon. 'You look all peculiar. Are you feeling sick or something?'

'I'm all right.'

'I said, who is he?'

'He's somebody called Arnold Luckett,' said James in an odd, distant voice that made Simon look curiously at him. 'Mr Arnold Luckett. And then it says the picture's by Frederick Ralston R.A. and he painted it in 1910. That's all.'

'Come on, then. Let's get it hung up.'

'Just a minute,' said James. He stared at Arnold's picture, and Arnold looked back at him, pinned behind the glass, for all the world like a benevolent walrus. Mr Arnold Luckett. A person with a gold watch-chain, giving money and things to schools. An important man. A serious man. James Harrison. Mr James Harrison. Arnold and James, down by the Evenlode, rabbiting and fishing and walking under trees through sunlight. Mrs Verity, plumped like a cushion into the chair on her front doorstep: a little girl locking the Vicar's sister unto the church hall, whooping and shrieking in the churchyard.

'Come on,' said Simon. 'What *is* the matter?'

'Nothing. I was just thinking.'

'What about, then?'

'People,' said James. 'People having layers, like onions.'

'You're daft,' said Simon. 'Plain daft. Mind out, you're going to drop your end if you don't watch it.'

They hung Arnold's picture above the long trestle-table in the main hall where he presided benignly over the Registers and Log Books and the school photographs of long ago. From time to time James glanced at the picture, as though he was looking for something, but after a while it became as though it had always been there, and he hardly saw it. In any case, the day was full of events and diversions: the arrival of a photographer from the Oxford Mail, visits from various people. Mr Hollings was in an exuberant mood. He had, for a joke, read out the Register for 1871 instead of 1971 and although there had been bewilderment among the children at least a dozen names had found someone to answer to them: the bun-faced children of the old photographs had gone, but there were new Slatters and Wasties and Lays in their place.

He examined Ledsham anxiously on the way home. The chemist's window had been mended, and the Vicar's front door scrubbed clean. And as far as he could see there were no further scars. Which, he thought, didn't mean much. Except, maybe, that Thomas Kempe was busy thinking up something else.

He passed Mrs Verity, sweeping her front doorstep and keeping an eye on the street. It must be, James thought, the most swept doorstep in Ledsham.

'Hello, dear. Toffee?'

'Thank you,' said James.

'You'll have been busy today, with this exhibition of yours.'

'Yes, very.'

'I'll be coming along tomorrow. I'd like to have a look. Take me back to when I was a girl. You like to remember, as you get older.' She stared over towards the Harrisons' front garden, where Helen was doing handstands against the front of the house. 'I could do that once,' she said reflectively. 'We'd do it out of sight though, in those days. It wasn't thought nice to show your knickers like that, for a little girl.'

'Oh,' said James, 'I see.'

Mrs Verity was silent for a moment. She seemed to be lost in thought. Then she went on. 'You think back. And often it seems more real than now. I mean, here I am, like this, but in my mind it's like I was different. Young, you see. You never really believe you're not any more.' She sighed, and looked at James, and James looked back and could find nothing to say that seemed at all useful, so he just nodded. He wondered if Mrs Verity was one of the smocked and booted girls in the photographs. And then all of a sudden something else occurred to him.

'Mrs Verity?'

'Yes, dear.'

'When you were at the school, can you remember somebody called Mr Arnold Luckett?'

'Mr Luckett? Oh yes. He was an old gentleman who used to come down from London every year. Very fond of Ledsham, he was—he used to spend his holidays here as a boy, I think. He had a gold watch on a chain, that I do remember.'

'Yes,' said James. 'That's right.'

'Why are you asking, dear?'

'Oh, I saw a picture of him today, that's all.'

'Ah. He gave us silver threepences, one each. And the teacher had us all shout "Three cheers for Mr Luckett." He'd have been past seventy, then.'

'Yes,' said James.

Mrs Verity sighed. 'Seventy-three I'll be, next birthday. It's a long time ago now. There's your mother at the gate, you'd better be getting along home, I daresay.'

'Goodbye,' said James. Mrs Verity went inside. The starlings sidled up and down her roof whistling and chattering.

The evening passed without anything in particular happening. James, though, was uneasy. The whole house had that feeling of time suspended which possesses a stretch of country before a storm, when trees stand motionless and there are no birds. At East End Cottage the rooms enclosed air that hung thick and heavy. People's footsteps made empty, ringing noises on the stairs and on the stone floors. Tim went under the sitting-room sofa and stayed there. Helen said, 'It's got stuffy now,

136

this house, instead of draughty,' and shut herself up in her room.

James went to bed early. He left the curtains undrawn and the window open to release the stifling pressure that filled the room. Outside, the church tower cut a dark block from the sky. A bright, hard moon came and went behind shreds of cloud. Mrs Verity's house was just a shape, except for the rim of light round a curtained bedroom window.

James wrote in his notebook, 'Treacle pudding for school dinner. Cottage pie at home. Only ate one helping because not properly hungry.' He stared at the sloping ceiling for a moment and then turned over the page to fill in his Future Plans, not because he had any in particular but because he liked things to continue as normally as possible. It came as not much of a surprise to find that Thomas Kempe had been there first. He had written, in small, crabby letters, not like his recent bold style:

I am wearie of this towne. There are people who practise strange thinges and I doe not understand their wayes.

James looked at this message for a long time. It seemed to be, in some way, an appeal, but he did not know what to do about it. And he was very tired. Too tired, in fact, to concentrate on it as he would have liked. The exercise book slipped out of his hand and flopped to the ground, and he fell asleep with the light still on.

He woke up suddenly and completely. Tim was barking, downstairs. And there was a smell coming in through the open window. It must be the very middle of the night. Tim was almost hysterical. And the smell ... He sat up. The mirror had writing on it, huge, soap or something. It said:

I HAVE BURNED DOWNE THE WYTCHES HOWSE.

He sprang out of bed and dashed to the window. The night
was clear and crisp and cold with the moon high now and
very bright and Ledsham dark and slumbering underneath,
the houses huddled together, their windows curtained and
blank. And there was this strong smell of bonfires, and a loud
crackling noise as though enormous fingers were rumpling
newspaper, and Tim, barking and barking downstairs ...

And then everything slammed into place in his mind, as it
would have done at once if he'd been quicker and not just a
bit blurred with sleep, and he was down the stairs and hammering on his parents' door and shouting, 'Wake up! Get up!
Dad! Mrs Verity's house is on fire!'

After that everything was confusion. Mr Harrison was tele-
phoning the fire brigade, and James and Helen were out in
the road in their night-clothes while Mrs Harrison banged on
Mrs Verity's door and up above smoke gushed from the thatch
and little spurts of flame and shoals of sparks drifted away into
the night. Mrs Verity, in a red flannel dressing-gown, came
out and was taken away to East End Cottage. Lights began to
snap on all down the street, and more people came out, and
went into the cottage and began to carry out Mrs Verity's
furniture so that in a few minutes the pavement underneath
the street light looked like a stall at a rather superior jumble
sale, heaped high with chairs and tables, and a canary in a
cage, and a pair of china dogs, and a loudly ticking clock.

And then the fire brigade came, and the whole operation was taken over by the stonemason from Bridge and Sampson, the builders, in his alternative role as the Chief Fire Officer, for the Ledsham Fire Brigade was one of those in which the fire-men are quite other people in real life, plumbers and butchers and farm workers. James had often envied them. It must be splendid, he thought, to be somebody mending a tap one moment, and then, at the blast of a siren, to be transformed into someone else in a uniform and high boots and a shiny helmet, riding high down Ledsham High Street on the side of the fire engine with everyone staring at you.

The street was filled with a maze of pipes and hoses. Two of the firemen disappeared into the cottage with axes in their hands, and others were pulling the thatch from the roof with hooks. Smoke welled up and the night became a soupy yellow colour. People coughed and moved back.

James found a fireman doing things with hoses and taps and said, 'Will the cottage burn down?'

The fireman shook his head. 'Not by the look of it. It's not got a proper hold. The roof'll have to go, but that'll be the worst of it. Lucky we come when we did.'

James raced back to his own house and reported this to Mrs Verity, who was sitting in the kitchen looking dazed and telling Mrs Harrison over and over again how she'd damped down the fire before she went to bed, that she was sure of, and the gas wasn't left on and she couldn't for the life of her think how it could have happened. Mrs Verity brightened up at the news and insisted on going outside again, and Mrs Harrison noticed for the first time that James was wearing neither dressing-gown nor slippers, so he put on his wellington boots over his pyjamas, because this was the nearest he could get to being a fireman himself, and went out into the lane again. On the way he stopped to congratulate Tim, who had, perhaps, been res-ponsible for saving the cottage, not to mention Mrs Verity herself. Tim, however, was unimpressed: he was busy harassing Mrs Verity's cat which, having been driven from house and home, was dementedly running up and down the wall.

There was more smoke and water about now than fire. The street was full of neighbours, most of them in dressing-gowns which was interesting in itself. You never, James thought, feel quite the same about somebody when you have seen them in their dressing-gown. Mrs Verity was sitting on the pavement in her own armchair, with a rug over her shoulders and the canary beside her, telling a group of people around her all about how she couldn't for the life of her think how it could have happened. Everybody was being very sympathetic and James had the feeling that in spite of everything Mrs Verity was going to get something worth having out of all this when it was over. It would be splendid for her to have a long, interesting story to tell to people in which she was the central figure, instead of just second-hand stories about other people.

The fire was rapidly being vanquished. There was no doubt about it. People were beginning to go back into their houses. Mrs Harrison found James where he had been sheltering behind the fire engine, hoping to remain unobserved, and said sternly 'James!' He went back into the house regretfully, and up to bed again. Mrs Verity came too, to spend the rest of the night in the spare bedroom. Outside, her possessions camped on the pavement and the firemen splashed around in the water that trickled from the pavement and ran away down the gutters, raking thatch from the roof and kicking away smouldering timbers.

'I can't bear to think of it,' said Mrs Verity, 'the mess there'll be.'

'Don't,' said Mrs Harrison. 'Leave it till the morning. We'll all feel stronger then.'

The fire, like any crisis, had provoked responses from everyone. People had stepped aside from themselves while it lasted and behaved differently. In the morning things seemed flat. Problems lay around like mountains.

'I talked to Mrs Trapp last night,' said Mrs Verity wonderingly. 'We've not spoken for four years last Christmas.' She looked across the road, and sighed, 'I'll not be straight again for weeks. It'll be a job to get the thatcher. I'll have to stop with my sister at Oxford till it's done.'

James, too, had had time to think about things. He was haunted by the thought of Thomas Kempe's earlier message. It had been a plea of some kind, he felt. Not a command, for once, but a plea. And he'd done nothing, and then the fire had followed, like some kind of desperate gesture. But what could he have done? What did the sorcerer want him to do?

Pondering all this, he made his way to school. He met Simon on the corner, and Simon talked excitedly of the fire.

'Is it true you discovered it?'

'Mmn,' said James.

'Cor! I wish it had been me. You don't seem very pleased.'

'It was him, you know,' said James. 'He did it.'

'Your ghost?'

James nodded.

'Oh,' said Simon. 'Do you really think so?' He went on, cautiously, 'The firemen were saying something about the oil-heater upstairs. Mrs Verity left it on and a window blew open and there was a draught.'

'They can think that if they want to,' said James. 'Nobody's stopping them.' He put his hands deep in his pockets and walked ahead, fast and alone.

It was the day of the centenary. The school was festive, and full of visitors all day. The people of Ledsham flowed in to look at the exhibition, see the school, and talk to the children. James, like the rest of the older ones, had a job to do showing visitors round and telling them about the work that they were doing at the moment. He spent a long time trying to explain a maths problem to an old lady who had difficulty with decimals and thought it was wonderful what children did nowadays, and an equally long time with Mr Dalton from the pub who turned out to be very interested in ancient Greece. But all the while, in one part of his mind, he was distracted. There was something required of him, but he did not know what it was. There was something he had to do, but he did not know how to do it. He stared at the portrait of Arnold, asking for help, but there was only Mr Arnold Luckett there, looking benevolent, with his gold watch-chain pulled tight across his stomach.

It was while he was on his own, looking at the old brown photographs and wondering which, if any, of the solemn little girls in white pinnies was Mrs Verity, that he felt Thomas Kempe. The sorcerer broke nothing, and slammed no doors, but James could feel him nonetheless. There was a constriction, a tightening of the air, but it was only for him: all around, people moved and talked unconcernedly. Mr Hollings hurried to and fro: a baby cried: someone called across the hall to a friend. 'What do you want?' said James, inside his head, and Thomas Kempe made a wall of air, as insistent as a wave at sea, and pushed James away from the table and into the classroom and then towards his own desk.

'What do I do?' said James, silently, and the lid of the desk rattled. He opened it, and the message was written on a piece of blotting-paper that lay on top of the exercise books.

Helpe me to goe. Finde my resting-place, & putt there my pype & my spectacles.

'Yes,' said James. 'Yes. I will. But you'll have to tell me where.'

He waited. He couldn't feel anything now. 'Where?'

143

Nothing.

'Do you mean,' he said carefully, 'the place where you were buried? Your grave?'

But Thomas Kempe wasn't there any more. There were just desks, and chairs, and pictures of Greek temples on the walls and the noise of people walking about and talking in the hall. James put the piece of paper in his pocket and went back to the exhibition, thinking.

He went straight home after school. Mrs Verity's house looked forlorn, the rafters of the roof bare to the sky and the front door locked. Mrs Verity had gone away to her sister's until it could be re-thatched. The starlings had moved to the telephone wires next door. James walked past quickly and into his own house. He went upstairs, took the pipe and the spectacles from the shelf where he had been going to make them part of his museum on Three Hundred Years of Domestic Life in an Oxfordshire Cottage, and put them in his anorak pocket. As he went past the kitchen door Mrs Harrison's voice said, 'Tea?'

'Later. I'm not hungry.'

'Are you feeling all right?'

'Perfectly,' said James.

He went along Pound Lane and then down Abbey Road and across the church square past the old lock-up. The sun was going down behind the Red Lion and the rooks were soaring and circling around the church tower, calling to each other and sometimes lifting away all together into the golden sky, only to come beating back a few minutes later. They roosted in the churchyard chestnut trees. James went round behind the church, through carpets of brilliant, papery leaves, and then stopped. He had forgotten there were so many gravestones. They reached right away to the point where the churchyard ended abruptly and the fields began, new ones and old ones, craggy, broken ones and hard marble ones, humble ones

144

and elaborate ones fenced in with black railings. Some seemed quite forgotten, half-buried under the turf, and smothered with ivy : others were banked high with flowers in jam-jars or even had rose trees growing by them, and tiny hedges planted around them.

There would not have been anyone putting flowers on Thomas Kempe's grave. I only need look at the old ones, he thought. The very old ones.

He worked his way slowly along. He climbed the black railings and stared at the elaborate barley-sugar carvings on the tomb of Samuel Brass, who Departed This Life in 1749 : he pulled the ivy away from the weeping cherubs on the grave-stone of Elizabeth Harley, Dear Wife of John Harley, Farmer, of This Parish : he peered until his eyes hurt to make out the faint names and dates on stone rubbed down and worn away by tens and hundreds of years of wind and rain and sun. And there were yet more that he would never be able to read : ancient, blunted stones whose inscriptions were altogether lost and whose very purpose seemed almost to have been forgotten, sinking as they were into the grass and leaf-mould in forgotten corners of the churchyard. Any one of these might be Thomas Kempe's.

James reached the very end of the churchyard. He looked despondently across the fields towards the Evenlode, winding away among willows between flat meadows. Then he looked back towards the church, standing square and sturdy on the edge of the town, looking, presumably, exactly the same as it had looked to Thomas Kempe, who disliked priests, but who, nevertheless, had required a piece of the churchyard in the end. But which piece? James felt suddenly very tired. He sat down at the edge of a rubbish heap. There was nobody else within sight, and no sound except the rooks, and somebody hammering inside the church.

The hammering went on and on, except that it wasn't

hammering, but a steel pick or something chipping away at masonry, and James looked gloomily at the gravestones and thought that there wasn't much more he could do. And then all of a sudden, for the second time that day, something clicked into place in his head. There was a person working in the church. And that person could only be Bert Ellison. And, all things considered, there was no one he would rather see just at the moment than Bert Ellison.

He ran back through the churchyard and into the church by the side door. Inside, there were rows of empty pews, vases of chrysanthemums, and long, dusty shafts of sunshine spilling down from the high windows above the nave. At the far end, invisible behind a pillar, Bert Ellison was whistling 'Colonel Bogey'. James walked down the aisle, and found Bert on his hands and knees beside a stone tomb in the small chapel along-side the altar. He was chipping out a flagstone. James said, 'Hello.'

Bert dusted his hands off on his overalls and looked up. 'I thought you'd be round one of these days,' he said. 'How's things, then? I saw your bloke had been up to no good.'

'You knew it was him? The writing on walls and all that?'

'I knew,' said Bert. 'But it wasn't any good going round and saying that, was it? There was those as would have agreed, but more that wouldn't.'

'Yes,' said James. 'That's what I thought, too.' He added, 'There was worse than that.'

Bert lifted a shaggy eyebrow. 'Worse?'

'The fire.'

Bert whistled. 'He had it in for her, didn't he. That could have been serious, that could.'

'I know,' said James. 'But something else has happened now. He wants to go.' He told Bert about the latest messages.

146

'And you've been looking out there for his grave, then?'

James said unhappily, 'Yes. For hours. But I can't find it. I don't see how you could.'

'No,' said Bert. 'You'd have a problem all right.'

'Why didn't he go when we were trying to exorcise him? Why now but not then?'

'Because he's an awkward cuss, that's why,' said Bert cheerfully. 'He don't want to be pushed around. Stands to reason, I suppose, being placed the way he is.' He sat back on his heels and pushed his cap back. 'I could do with a smoke, but it don't seem right, in here.'

'What'll I do?' said James. 'Just go on looking and looking?'

'I wouldn't do that. I think you'd be wasting your time. I've got a better idea. I could be wrong, but I've got a sort of a feeling he's not out there at all.'

James stared. 'Where, then?'

Bert tapped the floor with his pick. 'Down there.'

James looked at the floor, blankly, and then back to Bert.

'There's a vault,' said Bert. 'Under the floor there. It's got tombs in it. All them books about the church say it's been sealed for a few hundred years. But it hasn't.'

James looked down at the floor. There was nothing to be seen. It felt solid enough.

'I been down there,' said Bert casually. 'I went through by mistake last time I took these flagstones up to see what we could do about the damp. I got over-enthusiastic, as you might say, and went a bit too deep.'

'Didn't the Vicar know?' said James.

'I never mentioned it. There didn't seem to be any reason to, particularly, and he's a bloke that goes on about a subject rather, once you get him started, the reverend, so I just cemented it up again. But I did have a look round with a torch first, and there's some inscriptions down there and it's slipped my mind till this very moment but I'll swear one of them was some name very close to what you told me this bloke of yours calls himself.'

'I see,' said James. Then he said, 'And you mean you could sort of get over-enthusiastic and go a bit too deep again?'

'I could do that,' said Bert. They looked at each other, and then Bert took up his pick again and began chipping away round the edges of the flagstone.

James sat down on the steps of the tomb and watched. The light ebbed from the church. Shadows began to pack the roof and crowd around the pillars and dark oak pews. The knight and his lady lay on their tomb with worn faces and stiff stone drapery. He was a crusading knight, armoured from head to pointed feet, his hands frozen in prayer; he must have known strange, hot, far-away places, and then come back to die in Ledsham, among elms and willows beside the Evenlode. James fetched himself a hassock to sit on that had been embroidered by the ladies of Ledsham Women's Institute, and thought about this, and other things, and listened to the tapping noises of Bert's pick and watched the dust and chippings fly up around the flagstone.

'I think this is the one,' said Bert. 'I reckon it is.'

'What if someone comes?' said James.

'I'm seeing about the damp, aren't I?' said Bert. 'Rising damp, they've got here. I don't know anything about any vault.'

The church was very dark and quiet now, but not empty because no place that has been used for so long by so many people can ever be empty. Like all old buildings, it was full of their thoughts and feelings, and these thoughts and feelings seemed to crowd in upon James as he sat waiting and watching. He had asked Arnold to come, and Arnold had come at once and was there now, at James' elbow, waiting and watching with him.

'Here she comes,' said Bert. He put his pick down and

148

dug his fingers down under the edge of the flagstone. He heaved, muscles stood out like cords in his arms, the flagstone rocked, and tipped on to one side. James leaned forward.

'Hang on,' said Bert, 'I got to get through the next bit. I told you I mortared it up again.' He swung the pick down: the floor split, mortar crumbled away downwards, and there was a jagged black hole, man-sized.

'There we are,' said Bert. 'Let's have that torch.'

He pointed the torch down into the hole. 'Want to have a look?'

James clutched the edge of the stone step. He said to Arnold 'Shall I?' and Arnold told him he'd be a silly idiot not to. He got up, rather slowly, and came forward, and lay down on his stomach and shone the torch down into the hole.

It was smaller than he'd expected. A little, crumbling underground room, with rough masonry walls and rubble all over the floor. And long stone boxes stacked up on top of each other: several at one side, one by itself on the other.

Bert's face appeared at the other side of the hole. 'Let's have some light over here.'

James swung the torch round. They could see the lettering now on top of the solitary box, black-shadowed in the beam of light. 'I thought so,' said Bert.

Here lyeth ye body of
Thomas Kempe Apothecarie
he departed this life ye last of October AD 1629
in the 63 yeare of his Age.

'Apothecary?' said James. His voice dropped into the vault, sounding deep and hollow.

'He couldn't go having them put sorcerer, could he?' said Bert. 'Not if he wanted to be in here. The Church wouldn't hold with that.'

'Why do you think he wanted to be there?' said James in a

149

whisper. 'He wasn't very religious, was he? Believing in all that magic, and hating priests.'

'Ah,' said Bert. 'There's a lot of people like to hedge their bets, aren't there? Not all put their eggs in one basket. Then and now.'

There was a pause. 'Are you going down?' said Bert. 'Or am I?'

James said, 'I think I'd rather you did. If you don't mind.'

'Let's have the stuff then.'

James handed over the pipe and the spectacles and Bert swung his legs down into the hole. For a moment his body blacked out the light, and then he was down there and stooping over Thomas Kempe's tomb and his shadow made another Bert, flat and mobile, stretching itself over the floor and then bending backwards up the wall. Crumbs of mortar had showered down with him: James saw his large hand sweep them off the inscription and place the pipe and the spectacles side by side on the stone. And as he did so something happened along the edge of the yellow circle of torchlight: a little blue light came to join it, a pale, flickering light that slipped down the sides of the vault, climbed up Bert's leg, and then lay for a moment on the stone before it shrank to a pin-point and was gone.

Bert said, 'There. Give us a hand, can you.' He heaved himself out again and sat on the step beside James.

'Did you see?' said James. 'A light. It went out.'

'That's right.'

'Was it something to do with him?'

'I'd say it was.'

'Do you think that's that, then? He's gone?'

'I do,' said Bert, standing up and dusting down his overalls, 'I don't think you'll get any more trouble now. He's best off that way, too. He'd not got our outlook on things, as you might say. We do things different now, but you wouldn't have made him see that, not in a month of Sundays. Come on, you can help me fix this floor back.'

James looked down once more. It was too dark to see anything. For a moment there flashed through his mind the absurd notion that he might have put some flowers on the tomb. Which, in view of everything that had happened, seemed a pretty odd thing to think of doing. Bert must have been affected by the same sentiment for he said, 'I'd have liked to clean up a bit in there, but it's getting late. I like a memorial to be kept nice. There's not much else you can do for a person. Just remember their name and that.'

'I don't think I'll forget his name,' said James.

They re-sealed the hole. Bert dropped the flagstone back into place and filled up the cracks again so efficiently that any observer would have thought it had lain untouched for many, many years. Then he put his tools away and picked up the black bag. They went out of the church together and walked along the path towards the gate.

'I'm off home now,' said Bert. 'A bite of tea, and Match of the Day on the telly, that's me. Cheerio, son.'

'Cheerio,' said James. 'And thanks. Thanks very much indeed.'

'That's all right,' said Bert. 'You're very welcome. Any time.'

He took his bike from where it was leaning against one of the church buttresses, got on, and rode away out of the church-yard gates and out into the square. 'Colonel Bogey' floated back through the still evening air, along with the clank of the tool bag bumping against the mudguard.

James watched him go and then turned away to go home by the short cut through the churchyard and over the wall into Pound Lane. It was, he thought, the most perfectly splen-did evening he could remember. The sky was huge and clean and empty over Ledsham, a soft violet colour, with a feathery moon rising beyond the line of trees that fringed the church-yard. The trees were almost bare of leaves, their delicate branches splayed against the sky, loaded with the shaggy forms of rooks' nests. Above them, the rooks swirled and planed, rising and falling in invisible currents of air. James walked down the path and then under the trees. Grey, ribbed trunks reached up and up over his head to meet a canopy of branches that was like the vaulting of a cathedral, and from this roof came spinning down dozens and hundreds of leaves. He looked at the branches near his head and saw suddenly that the new leaves were already there, sharp folded shapes, shiny brown tips of beech and chestnut and elm. He walked on, with Arnold somewhere not far away, and the old leaves fell silently around him and piled up under his feet and above them the branches held up the new ones, furled and secret, waiting for the spring. Time reached away behind and ahead : back to the crusading knight, and Thomas Kempe, and Aunt Fanny, and Arnold : forward to other people who would leave their names in this place, look with different eyes on the same streets, rooftops, trees. And somewhere in the middle there was James, walking home for tea, his head full of confused but agreeable thoughts, hungry and a little tired, but content.

Penelope Lively

THE VOYAGE OF QV66

It was because of Stanley the voyage began. Pal the dog, Ned, Offa, Freda the cow and Pansy all knew what kinds of animals they were, but no one had *ever* seen anything like Stanley.

In a flooded world, from which humans have fled, this animal band voyages from Carlisle to London to find out just what Stanley is. Their only clue is a poster from London Zoo.

"brilliant comedy layered with meaning for many ages and tastes . . . Pathos, wit, suspense and intellectual toughness combine in Penelope Lively's superbly entertaining novel."

Margery Fisher, 'Sunday Times'

Penelope Lively

THE WILD HUNT OF HAGWORTHY

Lucy looks forward to summer in the country and to renewing her friendship with Caroline, Louise and Kester, the Blacksmith's son. But soon after she arrives, Lucy is troubled by the news that the ancient and long-forgotten Horn Dance is to be revived again at the summer fete.

As the participants rehearse in their old costumes and antlered masks, Lucy feels that sinister forces from the past are being unleashed and that the ghostly Wild Hunt will return – bringing with it a terrible danger . . .

"Narrative explodes into speed and terror before the shadows are beaten back."

The Guardian

"Telling descriptions of the Somerset countryside and excellent, funny modern dialogue combine with a very real supernatural to make a powerful whole."

The Times